MW01221948

EMBRACE THE HUNT

EMBRACE THE HUNT

Caris Roane

Copyright © 2015 by Twin Bridges Creations, LLC.

All rights reserved. No part of this Book may be reproduced in whole or in part, scanned, photocopied, recorded, distributed in any printed or electronic form, or reproduced in any manner whatsoever, or by any information storage and retrieval system now known or hereafter invented, without express written permission of the publisher, except in the case of brief quotations embodied in critical articles and reviews.

This is a work of fiction. Names, characters, places, and incidents are products of the author's imagination or are used fictitiously. Any resemblance to actual events, locales, or persons living or dead is entirely coincidental.

Formatting and cover by Bella Media Management.

ISBN-13: 978-1512378610

THE BLOOD ROSE SERIES
BOOK EIGHT

EMBRACE THE HUNT

CARIS ROANE

Dear Reader,

Welcome to the eighth installment of the Blood Rose Series, EMBRACE THE HUNT. In this book, Mastyr Ian joins forces with the Ruby Fae, Regan, to break down a deadly spell concealing the true scope of Margetta's army. But will they be able to overcome the effects of a terrible massacre that haunts each of their lives?

A powerful vampire warrior. A beautiful fae of great power. A war that threatens to destroy their love for the second time…

Mastyr Vampire Ian never wanted to see Regan again. He blamed her for the massacre at Raven's Overlook, an attack that killed his sister and her children. He's convinced Regan enthralled him, using her extensive fae powers to keep him by her side. If he'd been in his realm that night, he could have saved 200 people. Instead, he was caught up in a passionate affair with the woman known as the Ruby Fae. However, when the enemy abducts Regan, Ian goes on the hunt for her. Finding her trapped behind a wall of mist, he helps her escape the Ancient Fae's fortress. Reunited, old passions run hot once more, but will the past keep him from embracing the woman he's loved all these years?

Regan never stopped loving Ian even though they'd dated several centuries ago. But he'd always blamed her for the terrible events at Raven's Overlook. When she feeds him from her vein and learns she's a blood rose, she's devastated. Ian hurt her badly in times past by making her a scapegoat. But when she's forced to work alongside him to help battle the deadly Invictus wraith-pairs, her love for him rises once more. Yet, can she ever trust him again, when he swears she enthralled him that fateful night?

Enjoy!

Caris

For the latest releases, hottest pics, and coolest contests, be sure to sign up for my newsletter!!!

http://www.carisroane.com/contact-2/

Now Available: Rapture's Edge 1 Awakening, the continuing saga of the Guardians of Ascension, featuring Duncan and Rachel. He's a warrior to the bone, but she only wants peace!

http://www.carisroane.com/raptures-edge-1-awakening/

Now Available: Rapture's Edge 2 Veiled, the sequel to Awakening.

http://www.carisroane.com/raptures-edge-2-veiled/

Coming Soon, the final installment of the Blood Rose Series, Book 9, EMBRACE THE POWER. This story features Mastyr Stone as he battles Margetta, the Ancient Fae, for control of the Nine Realms.

http://www.carisroane.com/9-embrace-the-power/

Also coming soon, the first book of the Flame Series, BLOOD FLAME!

http://www.carisroane.com/blood-flame/

Be sure to check out the Blood Rose Tales Box Set – TRAPPED, HUNGER, and SEDUCED -- shorter works for a quick, sexy, satisfying read. For more information: http://www.carisroane.com/blood-rose-tales-box-set/

Chapter One

An hour from dawn, Ian sat in the dirt at the bottom of a dry streambed, head in hands, waiting for some sign Regan was still alive. With his ass on a couple of sharp rocks and a black scorpion not two feet away, he'd never felt so useless in his life than right now.

A slow-moving river ran through Dark Gorge another thousand feet below the streambed. When the rains came, this dry wash would spill a tall waterfall into the river.

Right now, it was as empty as his efforts to find Regan, the Ruby Fae.

He sat back and twisted his thumb ring. He had a ring on each digit, his way of dealing with shit. All but one of them symbolized the Nine Realms. The tenth ring, the one he turned to let off some steam, represented their world as a whole, which he worked night and day to keep safe.

He also used the heavy bling to beat the shit out of wraith-pairs. Maybe that was part of his problem; he hadn't been in a good fight for way too long. He enjoyed using his fists, going *mano-a-mano*.

Regan had disappeared from the Swanicott Fae Guild a month ago, abducted by the Ancient Fae. In truth, he didn't know if Regan was alive or dead. But each time he thought he might never see her again, something inside him tightened so hard he couldn't breathe.

She can't be dead. He didn't know what life was supposed to look like without Regan in it, even though she hadn't been a real part of his world for a long time. Yet some piece of her lived inside him, a heart beating alongside his own. He'd loved her once with a kind of madness he'd never experienced since.

And never wanted to again.

He lifted his head and stared up at the wall of mist at the top of the cliff. He wore sunglasses, and though it was still full-dark, he could see every detail as clear as day. For the past few decades, he'd become unusually sensitive to moonlight and at times even to the stars and for that reason had to wear shades.

But he could definitely see the mist, something only a handful of very powerful realm-folk could see. To most, the mist created an illusion that the mountain forest was right there and nothing else. What lay behind the mist, he didn't know, only that Margetta, the woman intent on taking over the Nine Realms, had created it.

He rose to his feet, but listed sideways. Spots hovered in front of his eyes. In his desperation to find Regan, he hadn't been feeding as often as he should. If he waited much longer, he'd fall into a coma and die.

When a crippling spasm hit his stomach, he knew he couldn't stay in the streambed a second longer. He'd have to suspend his hunt for Regan for the next fifteen minutes or so to take care of the problem.

Levitating swiftly, he flew above the gorge cliffs and headed to the outpost hamlet of Pikon. The small village was located where the cliffs dropped down to Leberion Plain, not far from the Peralin River.

Once he arrived, he flew down the short main street and saw that a light still blazed in the wrought iron lantern hanging outside the village inn. He landed on the walkway, but lurched forward to plant a hand on the heavy wood door in order to catch his balance. More spots moved back and forth in front of his vision.

Blinking several times, he removed his sunglasses to rub his eyes then put them back on. Even the lantern light hurt.

When he was steady, he jerked the door open and saw one of his regular *doneuses,* Charlotte, sitting on a bar stool in the pub. She wore rust suede, thigh boots, a short denim skirt, and a matching fringed jacket. She held a bottle of beer to her lips, but paused when she caught sight of him.

Setting the bottle down on the glossy wood bar, her eyes widened in shock. "Ian," she cried, sliding off her stool. "You've waited too long again. Sweet Goddess, open my vein now." She moved swiftly in his direction, her arms outstretched.

"Charlotte, thank the Goddess you're here." His gaze had settled on her pale throat, but he stumbled against her, losing his balance.

The lovely fae woman showed some sense and pushed him into the nearest booth. Given his size, he needed to make some room and used a booted foot to push the table to the opposite side. He was dizzy again, and fell backward onto the seat.

She landed on him, holding her long black hair away from her throat. "Dig in, mastyr. Take what you need."

As his fangs descended, he slid a hand around the back of her neck, tilted his head to the right angle then struck. Within a split-second, he was sucking down her blood.

The whole time his stomach cramped and only began to grow loose when it recognized the substance he needed so badly.

His thoughts however, flew straight back to the wall of mist that had for weeks prevented him from getting to Regan. He had to get back there.

He drank down the critical sustenance, counting the seconds. When he felt as though he could continue on without the risk of passing out, he released her neck and swiped the wounds with his tongue, healing them instantly.

"Mastyr, it's hardly been a minute."

"Got to get going."

"I'll stay here in case you need me." She called out to the troll innkeeper. "Will you stay open for him, Shayla?"

"Damn straight, I will. Anything for the Mastyr of Camberlaune."

When Ian rose to his feet, the dizziness was gone as were the spots that tended to float across his vision when his starvation became acute. He still felt weak as hell, though.

As Charlotte stood up, he placed a hand on her shoulder. "Thanks again."

She nodded, three quick dips of her chin. "I'm here to serve."

His lips quirked. "You were always my favorite."

At that, she giggled. "You forget, Mastyr, your *doneuses* compare notes all the time. You say that to each of us."

He smiled, adjusting his sunglasses. "Doesn't mean it's not true each time I say it."

His gaze dropped to the slight red patch on her neck where he'd suckled. His instincts told him to stay put and continue making use of Charlotte's vein, but Regan's plight called to him. He had to get back to the granite outcrop, to stand vigil, to wait, to hope, to pray she was still alive and he could help her.

~ ~ ~

An hour from dawn, Regan sat on the tall windowsill of her tower prison, her knees pulled up to her chest, her long gown wrapped around her ankles. While she waited for her last meal of the night, she looked out over the fortress grounds.

A large enemy encampment lay beyond the gray stone walls, made up of row after row of tents housing the murderous Invictus pairs. Yet, even as her gaze passed over the camp, she had a sense that a spell kept Regan from seeing everything that was there.

Margetta had placed her in the tower on purpose, giving her a view not just of the roof of the large stone fortress but of her army as well. Seeing so many Invictus pairs ready for war had a strong psychological effect. The thought that there might be more than even what she could see, had put a chill in her bones. Just how big was Margetta's army?

The Ancient Fae had painted a frightening picture of Regan's future as well. She planned to bond Regan with a mastyr vampire of her choosing, one aligned with Margetta. The vampire she'd chosen would not only rule Camberlaune, but would also serve as the leader of the entire Nine Realm's vampire community.

But, no, she hadn't named the man yet.

The only thing that surprised Regan was that Margetta hadn't already forced the bond.

In a moment of anger, Regan had asked sarcastically, "Why haven't you brought my husband to me? You must know I'm desperately lonely for company."

Margetta had lifted a lovely brow. "Don't you know? Your power has not yet been fulfilled. I only await the proper hour."

What hour? And what did she mean her power hadn't been fulfilled?

Margetta was a physically beautiful woman, with exquisite, wide-set, violet eyes, arched brows, a straight nose and softly pointed fae chin. She had long, blond hair worn throughout the past month in large curls to her waist. Except for the hollow expression in her eyes and the occasional malevolent smile, she looked like a princess from some of earth's fairy tales. She even wore long, velvet gowns around the fortress.

Regan knew the woman was monstrously ambitious but what troubled her more than anything was how calm she seemed. After all, she'd lost a huge battle in Swanicott Realm in which over two hundred Invictus pairs had either been killed or sent to Mastyr Ethan and Samantha for rehabilitation. Everything about Margetta's demeanor did not speak of a woman pressed against a wall and fighting for her existence.

Instead, Regan sensed the Ancient Fae was poised to accomplish what she'd been working toward for hundreds of years, from the time Margetta had created the first deadly Invictus wraith-pair.

When Regan heard the lock in the grate, she levitated slowly down to the tower floor. Though she was a fae with considerable power and had flown up to the sill, she wasn't strong enough to break through the iron lock on the heavy wood door.

She wore a soft linen gown, a garment Margetta had provided for her after telling her she'd burned Regan's 'disgusting' leather jacket as well as her jeans.

When she'd heard the news, Regan had quieted her emotions. She'd had that jacket for a long time, at least three decades. She'd tried it on just for fun at an open air market. In a moment of pure serendipity, Ian had seen her in it, a chance meeting never again repeated. He'd told her he loved the look on her.

The moment he left the stall, she'd bought the jacket, one of the few spontaneous purchases she'd ever made.

Now it had no doubt been tossed onto one of the many bonfires burning throughout the camp.

She'd even shed tears, which seemed absurd given her situation. Except the loss of her coat had been very symbolic; she had no protection against Margetta and very little control.

The door opened and the lovely fae-slave, Sandra, walked in. Behind her, but remaining in the doorway, was a very fat slave-troll with a dark look in his eye. He held the key to the tower door in his hand.

As soon as Sandra was inside, the troll shut the door and Regan could hear the lock turning in the grate. He then peered through the small barred opening to keep an eye on them.

Sandra kept her head bent and made no eye contact. In her hands she carried a tray bearing her second meal.

Regan had many times begged Sandra to help her, to bring her a key by which she might escape the tower. She'd even been encouraging Sandra to come with her, though she doubted this would be possible given the presence of the guard who always accompanied her.

But as Regan caught sight of the rolled up towel clutched tight beneath Sandra's arm, Regan's heartrate soared. Sandra never brought extra linens with her at this hour.

"As you requested last time, Mistress," Sandra said pointedly. "I brought a towel for you."

Regan had made no such request. "Thank you. I'm grateful you remembered. And how are you, Sandra?"

"Very well, thank you, Mistress." Her tone was breathy, as she slid her gaze to Regan and dipped her chin once.

She set the tray on the small table, then moved to the washstand. She tucked the towel next to a basin and companion water pitcher.

There could only be one explanation for the towel. Sweet Goddess, Sandra had brought the key.

In the month Regan had been imprisoned, she'd learned something of Sandra's history. She'd been imprisoned for thirty years and had served as a personal maid to Margetta all that time. Sandra had a sad aura that instinctively felt like more to Regan than just a reflection of her enslaved state.

Though Sandra had spoken only a little of her previous life, Regan knew she'd lost a husband and young son when she'd been abducted. Regan was pretty sure they'd died in an Invictus attack. But she'd never pressed Sandra for details. Again, her sadness had told its own tale.

Sandra represented for Regan all she despised in Margetta's regime. Worse, there wasn't a thing Regan could do for the slave.

By month-long habit, Regan sat down on the stool in front of the table. Sandra moved each item off the tray in a measured sequence of bowl and plate first, then embroidered cloth napkin, large spoon, and a small ceramic cup of blackberry wine.

Regan held her hands together in a tight clasp, her gaze never straying from the lovely braid draped over her Sandra's left shoulder. The young fae woman had beautiful red hair, a faintly pointed chin, dark eyes, and a smooth, delicate complexion.

Regan had to know, so she spoke mind-to-mind. *You brought the key? It's in the towel, right?*

For one of the few times in the month of service, Sandra smiled. *I did.*

Because Sandra was blocking the troll's view of Regan, she touched Sandra's arm. *Can you come with me? I'm a strong flyer.*

Sandra shook her head. *I might have my own way out. But if not, do all you can to take this monster down.*

Regan's eyes filled with tears. *I will. May the Goddess be with you.*

And with you.

No other words followed, just two tears tracking down Sandra's cheeks. She looked different somehow to Regan, maybe more confident. And she hoped with all her heart the slave would somehow make her escape as well.

Sandra took the empty tray from off the table and nodding to the troll, the key could once more be heard turning in the lock. When the door opened, Sandra disappeared into the small hallway beyond. The sounds of her steps as well as the troll's faded down the steep stairwell.

Regan moved to the door and listened intently. She would have to wait a few minutes, to make certain they were gone before she attempted her escape. Yet now that the moment was at hand, each second felt like an eternity.

When she sensed enough time had passed, she unrolled the towel and with trembling fingers picked up the key. Returning to the door, she slid it in the lock and after a couple of tries, felt it give way.

An enormous swell of emotion rushed through her and it felt like freedom.

~ ~ ~

When Ian reached the streambed, he didn't fly down to the bottom but crossed to the large outcropping of granite twenty feet away from the mist wall.

Regan, he pathed, using telepathy. *Are you there? Please answer me, sweetheart. This time, I beg you, please answer me.*

Though he hadn't received a single response in all these weeks, he still went through the drill, speaking to her as though she was there. *I've been here every night, hour after hour, since your disappearance from Swanicott Realm, since Margetta took you away from your home. Your servant witnessed what happened and I followed after you, but the trail ended here, though I'm not sure where 'here' is.*

I know I'm at the top of Dark Gorge and at the foothills of the Dauphaire Mountain Range. But I can't even see the mountains from here. Margetta has a spell in this area. I brought Ben here once to have a look as well, but he wasn't able to see the wall of mist, just me, and you know how much power Ben has. Ben said all he saw was the forest, but when I told him to enter the woods, he couldn't do it. He simply felt a tremendous urge to go the opposite direction, Margetta's spell is that powerful.

Regan, please answer me. Talk to me, Sweetheart.

He felt a sudden pressure on his telepathy. *Ian? Sweet Goddess, is that you?*

The sound of Regan's voice inside his head, set every warrior instinct on fire. He lowered his knees and stretched out both hands. His battle energy swept down his arms. If the Invictus came, he was ready. *Regan, are you okay? Is this really you?*

Yes, it's me. I'm trapped in Margetta's fortress, or at least I was. I'm outside now, but I don't know which way to go. The mist is so thick from here. When I was imprisoned in the tower, I could see for miles, but not now, not outside.

Ian felt both relieved and distressed at the same time. He'd been right all along; the Ruby Fae was here.

Regan, I can't move forward, because of the wall of mist. I'm on the granite outcrop above Dark Gorge. And where in the fortress are you exactly?

I'm on a catwalk, on the southern side. But the wall of mist is right there as well. Ian, Margetta has a large army here. I doubt even your Vampire Guard and Shifter Brigade combined could defeat it.

Ian took a moment to process this information. *Try not to think about that right now. It's more important to find a way for you to escape. We can deal with her army later.* But with so much adrenaline flowing through his system, he became acutely aware that the blood supply Charlotte provided him wouldn't last very long. *Shit.*

What? What's wrong?

Whatever we're going to do, we have to do it fast. My blood starvation is fucking me up.

She didn't respond right away, which probably meant she was thinking things through. *Don't leave yet, Ian. Please. I've waited a month for this chance and I have a feeling it'll be the only one I'll get. Margetta intends to marry me off to a mastyr vampire aligned with her, but she's waiting for some fulfillment of my power.*

Ian's heartrate ramped up as a long string of curses flipped through his head. Finally, he pathed, *I'm here.*

Waiting, however, became torture, since the spots had returned and once more flew before his eyes. He was worse off than he thought, but he couldn't leave her now, not when he'd finally made contact after all this time.

Regan, I'm going to try something. Focus on me as hard as you can. I want to see if I can home in on your telepathy and establish your location.

Oh, dear Goddess, Regan cried. *I can hear Margetta shouting. I don't have much time.*

Ian used what was left of his strength to reach through the mist with his mind, hunting for Regan. He had to find her and do it fast. For the helluva it, he added his battle vibration, stretching his hands toward the mist.

He'd been right to experiment because suddenly he found her. He couldn't see a damn thing, but he could sense her location fifty feet in the air, on the catwalk, but no more than a hundred yards almost directly in front of him. So close.

Staying focused, he found a path growing visible within his mind, the one that would take him to Regan. He'd be running blind through the mist, but without another thought, he headed into the spelled area and took each jagged curve of the path that presented itself within his head.

Regan, I'm coming to you right now. Be ready.

Margetta's not far.

He put on some speed.

As he moved, he brushed up against tree branches over and over, yet never once ran into anything. His path was true.

When he reached his destination, he could finally see the gray stone walls of the fortress right in front of him. Looking up, the mist still cloaked the higher reaches.

Ian!

He shouted telepathically, *Levitate straight down. I know you can't see anything, but I'm right below you.*

I hope to hell you are.

Have faith, but keep pathing to me.

I'm jumping now. Ian, find me. Find me fast.

But he could feel her as if he was actually looking at her. He held out his arms and only during the last second of her leap, did he finally see her. She landed in his arms, and he caught her against his chest. *I've got you.*

She clasped him hard around the neck. *Thank you.*

We've got to get out of here. With nothing to home in on for the return trip, he rose high into the air above what had to be the forest canopy. He then headed in a southerly direction toward Dark Gorge.

The moment he broke free of the mist, he was surprised to find he'd flown a full quarter mile up into the air.

He began a quick descent, however, knowing Margetta would give chase. The moment he dropped below the cliff edge, he could breathe easier.

Spots, however, started flying in front of his vision again, reminding him how far he'd pushed his blood starvation. For a moment, his levitating skill faltered.

Ian!

Regan's voice brought him around, and he had just enough left in him to regain his balance. He flew swiftly toward the Peralin

River and finally landed them both on the opposite bank in a nest of shrubs, deep in the gorge.

All went black.

~ ~ ~

Regan brought herself to a sitting position. The landing had been hard and she was bruised, but safe.

She worked at clearing her head. *Ian?*

But nothing returned.

He lay sprawled on his back, his sunglasses gone. His usual golden complexion had paled and his eyes were closed. She'd never seen him look so bad.

She knew he was close to coma, after which death would follow swiftly. All mastyrs were cursed with this kind of chronic condition, but she didn't know why Ian had let himself get to such a dangerous state.

Her mind made a swift adjustment. She drew her wrist to her lips and using her teeth tore through a vein. She cried out in pain, but she had to do it.

She forced his mouth open, then placed her arm over his lips, stroking his throat. *Ian, drink. Please, take my blood.*

Her veins released their nourishment readily and at first he gagged and choked. But when he finally got some of her blood into his stomach, his eyes fluttered open and he grabbed her wrist, forming a seal.

He was wild-eyed as he suckled.

And it hurt, but she didn't care. She'd made it out alive and Ian would live. Each had come so close to death.

She glanced over her shoulder. Through the shrubbery behind which she was hidden, she could see a golden glow at the top of the gorge.

Margetta had followed them.

Though a thousand feet distant, the Ancient Fae was no doubt searching the shallow bank along the river. Regan wasn't sure Margetta would actually be able to see them, but she didn't want to risk being caught.

We have to leave, she pathed to Ian. *Margetta is standing on the outcropping staring into the gorge.*

Does she have Invictus with her?

No.

Then, we're out of here.

Ian became one fluid movement as he pulled her against him, while holding her wrist tight to his mouth. He swept her swiftly downriver, flying close to the water through Dark Gorge. Faster and faster he went as her blood restored him.

Ian was one of the most powerful vampires in all the Nine Realms. Even if Margetta chose right now to summon Invictus to chase them, they'd never catch up.

Regan faced forward as Ian flew her to safety. Dark Gorge was one of the wonders of the Nine Realms. It spanned both Camberlaune and Tannisford Realms as did the Dauphaire Mountain Range. The length of the gorge was nearly two-hundred miles with a high plain on the southern slope and the tallest mountains of all the realms on the northern side. Because not all realm-folk could fly, dozens of bridges spanned the gorge.

With one arm wrapped around Ian's neck, she couldn't remember the last time she'd been this close to him. But it had to be centuries. She could feel his numerous thick rings as he held her wrist to his mouth.

The sensation of his suckling sent shivers of desire all along her arm. Being this close, she sniffed his skin at his neck. His cologne reminded her of the forest, deep in the darkest places where the soil was rich with life-giving humus. She wondered what it was called. Whatever it was, it did something to her and she might have to buy a bottle just to enjoy the fragrance now and then.

She couldn't believe she was here, in Ian's arms, or that she'd escaped the powerful Ancient Fae.

For a month, she'd lived under Margetta's rule and some of that time had been physically painful. Now she was flying through Dark Gorge and she was safe.

Tears of relief and gratitude stung her eyes. She took deep breaths to calm her spirit and silently sent prayers of thanksgiving to the Goddess.

She also couldn't have done it alone. *Thank you for being there, Ian. I'd still be a prisoner otherwise. Thank you so much.*

You're safe. That's all that matters.

Though she sensed he was no longer in danger of sliding into a coma, she was glad that as he flew he continued taking down her life force.

After a moment, her thoughts turned to the first day of her imprisonment. Though it wasn't the most significant thing that had happened, it had meant everything to her. *Margetta burned my clothes when I arrived, including my coat.*

Continuing to suckle steadily, Ian pathed, *The black leather one you were wearing when I saw you in Swanicott?*

Yes.

Was it the same coat you were trying on at the open air market, what, thirty years ago?

She turned her face toward him a little. *I'm stunned you remember. But yes, that's the coat.*

He chuckled, a low seductive sound that reached into her chest and grabbed her heart. *I watched while you bought it then put it on for good. It looked great. You know that's something I always liked about you. Here you were this serious fae teacher, almost a prophet among the Fae Guild circle. Yet you didn't mind wearing black leather and a lot of make-up. I always thought you'd look good on the back of my Harley.*

Her hand touched his bare shoulder, reminding her he never wore the traditional woven shirts all Guardsmen sported. The Guard coats hung to mid-calf but were sleeveless. *I had no idea you'd stuck around to watch me.*

Oh, I did. Had a good long look. I almost headed back in your direction about a dozen times. Now here we are, flying down Dark Gorge together.

Yep, here they were, but she had no idea what would happen next. They'd spent the last few centuries in strained silence because of their previous relationship. It had ended with a lot of blame on his part, and heartache on hers. Now he'd rescued her from Margetta's fortress.

We're getting close to my house. You've never been here, have you?

No, never. But I heard Zane talk about it a lot, especially when the house was under construction. I understand Mastyr Seth inspired you.

He did. Absolutely. Though half my home sits on solid rock. Seth's hangs off the side of the Walvashorr gorge. I also have a view of the mountains beyond and as I recall Seth's is smack up against the forest.

It is.

When he began to slow, she knew they were nearing his house, or one of them. Most mastyrs kept several houses around the realm for security.

He finally released her wrist, but held onto her arm to keep her balanced against him. She had both feet settled on his right boot and felt perfectly safe. Of course, she had the ability to levitate as well, so she wouldn't fall very far if she lost her hold on him. But she couldn't fly nearly as fast as Ian.

He was a big man, just shy of Mastyr Jude's extraordinary mass. And for a brief moment, her mind flew back, all those centuries ago, when they'd been lovers. How much she'd delighted in his body. He'd often laughed at her, at the way she touched him and did other things, saying she made a full meal of every muscle he possessed.

And so she had. But what woman with a grain of sense, finding herself with such a banquet beneath her fingertips, wouldn't take the time to explore and enjoy?

Of course these were hopelessly errant thoughts. She had no intention of taking up with Ian again, not when he'd hurt her so badly. But was she tempted? Sweet Goddess, *always!*

Yet, she'd kept her physical distance. He'd made his harsh opinions clear to her all those years ago and hadn't changed his view of her character even a little.

But being this close to Ian, brought the best parts of their relationship fully back to mind.

When he slowed to a hover, then eased around a final bend in the gorge, she saw the house perched on an outcropping of gray striated granite. He'd built his home on the curve of the terrain so that from one side of the house there would be a unique view of an angled stretch of Dark Gorge. The eastern view took the eye all the way to the Leberion Plain.

You built very close to the Dauphaire Rim.

I did.

The geography of the land had steep cliffs in a two-hundred-mile stretch across much of Camberlaune, all angling slightly to the plain below. The region where the cliff was visible from the plain was called the Rim.

Ian pathed. *I wanted to be close to the largest portion of the population, yet in the center of the realm geographically. This seemed like the best choice. And I love the view of the mountains, the gorge and the plain.*

Are there still only scattered settlements in the mountainous areas?

Yes, on either side of the gorge, shifters mainly. A few trolls. A bulk of the men are strong warrior types and belong to my Shifter Brigade. They do most of the higher elevation patrolling. The Invictus attacks are heaviest on the plain where the population is the densest, especially closest to the Rim. Although until Margetta kidnapped you, I didn't know her fortress was on the border between Camberlaune and Tannisford.

She felt the weight of his comment like a drag on her soul. He was mastyr of his entire realm and like all the realm rulers, he carried the burden of his people's safety. She wondered if she'd ever truly understood what ruling was like for him.

She felt a shudder run through him and she wasn't surprised when he said. "It'll be dawn soon."

Any vampire caught in the sunlight would die within minutes. Fae were also sunlight sensitive, though not as instantly harmed as vampires. She would survive a few hours longer than Ian, though not by much. So, she, too, could feel the hour was coming when they would need to seek shelter.

I'm afraid you'll have to stay here through the day. I know you'd rather be home in Swanicott, but I have a guest room you can use.

She chuckled softly. *You could tell me I had to sleep under a haystack for the day and I'd be completely content. Your home is more welcome to me than you'll ever know.*

When thoughts intruded of all that had happened during her month's imprisonment, she set them aside. There would be plenty of time in the future to deal with the ways Margetta had tortured her.

Ian flew her to what proved to be the main entrance, though on the eastern side of the round, cliff-edge dwelling. Landing on a gravel drive, he led her up several wide stone steps. The front door was arched and made of clear glass with an intricate, protective metal design crisscrossing the outward facing side.

"I love this door," she said, running her hand along the curves of one of the central metal supports. "It's almost like something you'd find in the forest, like entwined branches."

He opened the door for her. "When the architect showed me the design, I had the same response; it had the feel of the nearby mixed forest, especially some of the deciduous trees now that they've lost their fall leaves."

She moved into the foyer, remembering just how much Ian's warrior nature had a strange companion sensibility that her fae soul loved. Ian had even studied architecture at one time, though a couple of centuries ago. Taking in the lines of the house both outside and now within, she saw this side of his abilities in the complex design of the modern dwelling.

As he closed the door behind, a sudden whirring sound moved through the house.

"What is that?" She turned in a quick circle, wondering if they were under attack.

"It's only the steel shutters. I wanted extensive views for this house which meant a lot of windows. In turn, I installed a system of heavy screens to come down automatically at dawn."

She had her hand to her chest and tears touched her eyes. "I'm sorry."

He took hold of her arm in a gentle clasp. "For what?"

She squeezed her eyes shut for a moment, remembering how difficult it had been to get used to being imprisoned in the fortress. "I didn't mean to sound so alarmed when the screens descended. The first week in the tower, I jumped at every strange knock, jangle, or creepy wraith-shriek. And there were a lot of those. I'll calm down eventually."

He held her gaze, his dark gray eyes full of concern. "Did she hurt you?"

Regan nodded. "She had a way of burrowing into my mind and causing pain."

"Often?"

"The first week, yes."

"Did she have a purpose? Did she want something from you?"

Regan slid her fingers into her hair, shaking her head. "I have no idea. She was so strangely composed the whole time. I think she was toying with me for her own amusement."

Ian stood with his hands on his hips, frowning heavily, his gaze still fixed to her. In that position, each of his rings stood out because he'd made fists. They were all silver but none were the same, just heavy with a deadly feel.

"I hate that she had you imprisoned. I've died a thousand deaths out there, hoping, praying we'd connect, that I'd be able to get you away from her."

She tilted her head. "Ian, have you been near the fortress all this time, since I was abducted?"

He nodded. "From the time I located the mist and that was two days after you were taken."

She looked into smoky gray eyes, so familiar to her. When he would make love to her, he always held her gaze and she'd loved it. She'd forgotten how handsome he was in his rugged way. He had broad cheekbones angling to a strong jaw. His lips were full and his nose somewhat hawkish, especially when he flared his nostrils like he was now.

"Are you wearing perfume?" he asked.

She had to laugh. "I've been in a tower prison, remember?"

"Right." His frown deepened and his hand shot to his stomach. "Oh, shit. No."

She reached out and touched his shoulder, his skin warm against her fingers. "What's wrong?"

His gaze shifted back and forth over her eyes. "How do I smell, right now? To you?"

She shrugged slightly, then smiled. "I used to take long walks into the forest behind the Fae Guild retreat. My favorite path took me maybe three miles away from the compound. It was so deeply shaded that at night even my fae vision had a hard time warming it up so I could see. But the smell in that particular location was very dense and rich, full of humus, the kind you'd collect to feed your garden. That's what I'm getting from you right now, a rich forest scent, where ferns live and where the soil could grow anything. So what kind of cologne is it?" She was smiling at him, but he looked frighteningly sober in return.

He narrowed his eyes. "And was that true a few centuries ago, when we were together? Did you smell this cologne on me then?"

"No. You never wore cologne, even though you could have. I know that some of the elven population were quite adept at blending fragrances all those centuries ago." She forced her mind to flow backward, recalling the intensity of their relationship, of making love with him and savoring every part of his body. She shook her head several times, needing to dispel the memories. She could feel her desire for him rising the longer she stood so close to him.

"I still don't wear cologne, Regan. It's not my thing."

He didn't say anything more, yet his silence forced her to consider.

Her gaze fell to his hand on his stomach, and she finally got the picture. "Wait a minute. No. Ian, no. This can't be. Oh, sweet Goddess. Tell me you're not free of pain."

"Yes, and that makes you—"

"A blood rose."

At that, he turned away from her and let go of a long string of obscenities. "This is why I was so obsessed. Why I had to follow after you. Why I stuck around at the wall of mist." He wasn't looking at her as he spoke, but had turned toward the living room. Steel shutters now covered several broad panels of glass, leaving the space as though it was still night. With her fae internal clock, she could tell the sun was close to breaching the horizon. She couldn't leave now if she wanted to.

"What do you mean, obsessed?"

He held his hands wide. "The only person I brought to the granite outcrop was Ben and even then I felt uneasy because he was there. I wouldn't let anyone else come with me while I waited at the gorge. I told Ben it was because I needed him to take charge of the Vampire Guard, but it always felt like more, like I didn't want him or any other vampire near you."

Tears bit her eyes as she glanced once more at his stomach.

"Hey, I didn't mean to upset you."

"It's not what you think. I'm just suddenly so grateful you no longer have pain. And I was able to do that for you." All mastyr vampires suffered crippling stomach agony as a result of chronic blood starvation. She'd fed him often back when they'd been together, but he'd never been free of pain as he was now.

She shook her head, the truth of her situation hitting her hard. She was a blood rose and so long as she fed Ian, he'd never experience his previous suffering again.

But she didn't want a relationship with him either. There was too much contention between them for that. Yet, she cared about him and would as long as she lived. "You can always open my vein, Ian, anytime you want. No matter what happens."

He faced her again. "It won't be that simple. I saw what having a blood rose did to Zane and I've talked to several of the mastyrs. And now that I'm feeling the effects of this phenomenon—"

Without warning, he drew close and gathered her into his arms. He levitated, lifting her at the same time, then moved her into the hall, pushing her up against the wood paneling.

Connecting his hips with hers, he said, "This is the problem."

The linen gown she wore, with not even a thong to add another layer between herself and Ian's leather pants, allowed her to feel the full length of his arousal.

Oh, sweet Goddess, she was in trouble. "Ian, don't."

"Don't what? Don't feel what I'm feeling? Right now you smell like a flower, like jasmine, but there's a citrusy lime scent as well. And I've got a cloud in my head instead of a single rational thought. And only one drive." He ground his hips against her.

Regan hadn't been this close to Ian in such a long time. She put her hand on his cheek, her gaze falling to his lips. Would it be so bad to surrender to what she felt, to the strength of the emotions racing through her? Her body called for him, longing for him. But there were too many memories. "We fought badly, remember?"

A haunted look entered his eyes. "Something I try to forget and haven't in all this time." He eased away from her.

"You blamed me." Her chin rose and some of her desire started sliding away. "You were so angry. You never forgave me for the massacre at Raven's Overlook."

With these words, Ian planted his hands against the wood paneling, his jaw moving back and forth. "None of the mastyrs had ever lost an entire village to an Invictus attack, not before or since. Yet, I did. My sister and her two daughters died as well." He pushed away from the wall but pounded his fist against the paneling at the same time.

If his words hadn't convinced her, his behavior did: Ian still hadn't forgiven her. She doubted he ever would.

"Ian," she called to him sharply, commanding his attention. When his gray eyes grew fixed on her, she said, "Just for the record,

I did nothing wrong. You shouldn't have blamed me for what happened."

"But it was all your fault!" he shouted, his face turning a dark reddish hue. "You had me enthralled with your fae abilities and because of it, I shirked my obligations to the realm-folk of Camberlaune. I should have been with my Guard that night. Instead, I was in Swanicott mooning around your feet."

And that's how he saw it all, that she'd enthralled him leading him to forfeit his duties. But his anger, and completely misplaced judgements, fueled her own rage.

Straightening her spine, she lifted her chin. "You can't control the tides, Ian. You never could. We were two people in love. Ben had charge of the realm that night; you'd left everything in capable hands. But because the absolute worst happened, you chose to believe the worst of me and to blame me. But you're wrong about all of it and I resent the hell out of you for it." Her own face flamed now and his deep, earthy scent faded along with her desire. "Now, show me to your guest room, because I want a shower and then a long day of nothing but sleep."

Chapter Two

Despite her insistence on not needing anything but sleep, Ian offered her a sandwich, or anything else she might want, but she refused. Apparently, Margetta had fed her well, even if she'd tortured her.

He led her to his guest room, opposite the master bedroom, expressing his hope she slept well. She thanked him, though her tone was chilly.

He left her and grabbed a glass of sweet, German wine, afterward heading to his library. He sometimes sat among his books, looking at the scenery before retiring for the day. After what Regan had said to him, he'd needed something to calm him down.

But like hell she wasn't to blame.

If he hadn't been enthralled, he would have been patrolling Camberlaune that night. He was convinced he could have prevented the massacre.

He sighed heavily. The room faced northwest and since the sun never hit the windows in this part of his home during late fall and winter, the shutters hadn't come down. The window had a curve to it because of the disk-like shape of his house. With the bend in the gorge he could almost see the river below.

The sky was blue now, the sun having risen well past the skyline. He had a view of snow-capped mountains, dotted at the lower elevations with evergreens and the bare branches of elms and chestnut oaks.

He frowned and touched his face, then blinked his eyes. Where were his sunglasses? He must have lost them when he flew Regan to safety over the river.

He blinked again, several times, expecting to experience the sharp darting pain he'd known for years. But it wasn't there. The pain was gone, just like the cramps in his stomach. He could look at blue sky and his eyes didn't hurt. Unbelievable.

He shook his head. He couldn't remember the last time he'd set his gaze at a sunlit vista without cringing in pain. A lot of the vampires he knew, once well away from direct sunlight, could enjoy all kinds of scenery.

When he'd first become afflicted, he'd sought out a powerful fae healer. But all she could tell him was that it was part of his mastyr suffering, unique to him. And somehow, tapping into Regan's vein, had corrected the problem.

He still couldn't believe she was a blood rose.

He also felt the whole thing a cruel irony since the woman who'd cured him with her blood was someone he could never be truly connected to.

He knew he needed his bed. He was tired, not just from the night's vigil, but from a month of stress, of worrying about Regan, of not knowing if she was even alive. But there were a couple of tasks he needed to get done before he could make his way to the master bedroom.

He pulled his cell from his pants pocket and called Ben.

"Ian. Been waiting for your call. Everything okay?"

For a moment, Ian didn't know how to answer the question. Having fought with Regan before he'd been with her even half an hour, had left a sour taste in his mouth.

"I've got Regan with me. She escaped Margetta's fortress and yes, she's fine."

"That's great news. I'm relieved. Have you let Mastyr Zane know?"

"My next call."

"Good. Good."

"How's Camberlaune?"

"The usual number of Invictus sightings through the night, but the Guard and the Shifter Brigade performed as expected. We only had one injury, with dozens of casualties on Margetta's side. And we were able to send nine Invictus pairs to Ethan and Samantha for separation and rehab."

Ian wanted to rejoice; this was all good news. But a stone sat on his heart. "Glad to hear it."

Ben fell silent for a long moment. Ian's gaze had settled on a chokeberry shrub twenty feet from the window. A red cardinal was flitting around like he was lost, then suddenly darted away.

"All right, mastyr, what's going on?"

Ian shook his head. Ben could read him better than any of the Guardsmen or even any of the other ruling mastyrs. Of course, Ben was at mastyr level himself and not far behind Ian in power, which meant, yeah, he could read Ian. "I've just learned Regan's a blood rose. And before you congratulate me, believe me, this sucks."

Ben remained silent for several beats. "Are you kidding me? Why, Regan, of all women?"

Something inside Ian relaxed. Ben understood the nature of the dilemma.

Ben continued. "Oh, shit."

"What?"

"I just realized I won't be able to be around her."

"Unless you're interested in bonding with a blood rose."

"Not funny, Ian."

"No, it isn't."

Once more, Ben grew quiet. Ian knew his best friend needed to process the information as much as Ian did. The attack on Raven's Overlook had taken the life of Ben's older brother as well, a devoted Guardsman named Sean.

But Ben had never faulted Regan for the massacre. If anything, he'd taken responsibility for the disaster himself. He'd been on duty and somehow he'd misread the Invictus movement that night and an entire village had died.

But Ian had never thought for a moment Ben was to blame. And so help him, as long as he had breath, one day he'd make Regan see how she'd been in denial for five long centuries.

"Listen, Ian, get some rest. You've had a shitty month. And whatever you might think of Regan, she's served the Nine Realms faithfully for a long time and I'm glad she's okay. Call me later when you're up for the night. I'll be happy to take charge of the Guard and the Brigade for however long you need. My guess is Margetta will be on the hunt for Regan."

"Thanks, Ben. Can't tell you how much that means to me. But before you go, there's one thing I'd like you to do for me." When he delivered his request for Ben to find a replacement jacket for Regan, Ben said he'd see what he could do.

When Ben hung up, Ian spent the next several minutes talking with Zane of Swanicott, reassuring him that Regan was well. He also told him what Regan had said about the size of Margetta's army, to which Zane whistled low and added one powerful 'motherfucker'.

"What's the plan?" Zane asked.

The question was logical, but Ian's brain wasn't functioning at top speed. He swirled his wine in the clear glass goblet. "Hell if I know. I'm still adjusting."

"To Regan in your house?" Zane was also a good friend and had asked the right question.

"That and something else." He didn't want to speak the words aloud again, but he needed to face up to his new reality, the sooner the better. "Regan's a blood rose."

Zane responded as he had before and another beautiful 'motherfucker' left his lips. "And Regan, of all women. Yet, I don't know." He paused, then, "It feels right to me."

"Since when are you 'feeling' anything, my friend?"

Zane laughed, a deep resonant sound he hadn't heard in maybe the whole of Zane's life. "Since Olivia, that's when. Sweet Goddess, that woman can make me laugh. And I see a lot of things differently now."

"No, shit." Ian didn't think he could handle much more of Zane's current positivity gained from his recent bond to his own blood rose.

He frowned as he settled his elbow on the arm of his leather chair. He rubbed his forehead with his thumb, then looked at the etched silver rings he wore. "I'll say one thing. It's incredible not having pain."

"I'm with you there." Zane paused for a moment, then lowered his voice, "Ian, it's not so bad having a blood rose enter your life.

There's a certain amount of mystery to the process. I can only say Olivia changed just about everything for me, and all of it good. Try to be open to Regan if you can, though I know, given your history, it would be tough."

Zane didn't know the half of it. "Yes, it would. But I wanted you to know I've got her and she's safe. I'll probably bring her back to Swanicott later this evening."

"You do what you gotta do."

~ ~ ~

Regan held the edge of the blanket between her index and middle fingers, rubbing back and forth. She'd soothed herself this way from the time she was a child. The shower had been heaven, and her escape from Margetta's fortress was a wave of relief that kept delivering.

Her hair was damp as were her cheeks. She wasn't even sure why she wept. Maybe for Sandra and the rest of those enslaved by Margetta. But also because she'd fought with Ian and because he'd never forgiven her for something she hadn't done.

She doubted he ever would.

He believed she'd bewitched him in some fae-ish way, though she hadn't. She'd never done anything like that in her life and never would. Unlike the powerful Vojalie, who could enthrall easily and take over the minds of those less powerful than herself, Regan's ability was quite limited.

His accusations had cut deep for so many reasons. How could he have known her all the months they'd been lovers, yet not really *known* who she was, her integrity, her innocence?

She wiped at her tears some more.

She wasn't sure she'd be able to sleep. She threw back her covers, and though Ian had given her one of his freshly laundered t-shirts to sleep in, she needed something else.

Roaming the house, she went into the living room and found exactly what she was looking for. A small leather pillow with a crinkled texture sat against the gray wool sofa back.

She picked it up and pressed it to her nose.

There it was, the rich, deep forest and fern scent that she'd smelled earlier.

She returned to her bedroom and closed the door tight.

Crawling back into bed, she dragged her nose across the leather once more, then held the pillow to her chest.

Within a few minutes, she was sound asleep.

~ ~ ~

That night, as Ian sat in the kitchen, he heard Regan's footsteps in the hall, then heard her call out, "What's this?"

He lifted his head from the Camberlaune Chronicle, shifting his gaze to her as she drew close to the marble island. She held up the new soft black leather jacket, the one he'd asked Ben to hunt down for him. For a last minute's notice, Ben had done well. Of course, he had several trolls on his staff who'd probably done the leg work during the day given that trolls had no aversion to sunlight.

"You mean the jacket?"

"Well, yeah. Where did it come from? It looks almost identical to the one Margetta took from me."

Regan looked amazing in her snug jeans and leather ankle boots. Her braided belt had cinched in her waist to a perfect hand-measuring size and he wanted his hands on her.

He'd awakened with an arousal so hard, he'd stayed in one position for a long time just trying to breathe. The urgency he'd experienced to cross to the guest room and take the woman in bed then and there still had his thighs in a restless state.

Even now, just looking at her and catching her sweet jasmine and lime scent, had him shifting in his seat and trying to get more comfortable. The needs of his cock fused with his mind, and he knew words of any kind wouldn't come easily. Despite the handicap, he struggled on, forcing his mind to put a few sentences together. "Uh, the jacket. Yeah. I told Ben what happened and he found this for you." He waved at the coat. "Hope it's the right size. Olivia sent over the rest of your clothes and make-up. Everything okay?"

She frowned. "Everything's fine." She lowered her hand and stared at the jacket. "Great, really. And I do appreciate this."

"Uh, good." He repressed an eye-roll at his inability to properly express himself. But he couldn't get over how pretty she looked with her smoky lavender eye-shadow swept to a point on each lid and her brows arched and dark with whatever women did to their eyebrows. He could tell she'd worked on her hair. It was poufy, the way she liked to wear it and had a sort of wave in back, in fact a few waves.

His gaze fell to her lips. She'd always had beautiful, full lips, and they gleamed with gloss, or at least he was pretty sure that's what she called it. He wanted to spend some time getting it off her, taking some onto his own lips.

"Thanks for the compliment and the jacket," she added, though her frown had deepened. She lay the jacket over the back of the nearest bar stool. "You're acting kind of weird."

He shook his head. "I feel weird. I don't have any pain and my eyes don't hurt anymore."

Her arched brows rose. "They don't?"

"Not even a little. Another side benefit of your recent donation, I guess. Want some coffee?" He rose as he spoke, and picked up a white ceramic mug, waving it in her direction, waiting for her decision.

"Uh, sure. Yes. Absolutely. Sweet Goddess, the swill Margetta served. It tasted like she rolled the beans in the mud before grinding them."

He crossed to the coffee maker and poured her a cup. "You'll like this, then. I have a colony of trolls in the mountains who do nothing but grow coffee beans. The Guardsmen take turns making sure the Invictus don't bother them. We're all addicted."

He handed her the mug, which she took in both hands. Taking her first sip, she moaned softly.

The sound was unfortunate. He still remembered all the noises she could make when he had her in bed, from the softest coo to the throatiest groan. Of course, the utterances had nothing to do with tasting coffee and everything to do with his need to sit down again and try to ignore her or at least her damn womanly scent.

Goddess help him.

"I'm taking you back to Swanicott at full-dark."

Her brows rose. "You think that's wise?"

He drew a deep breath, trying to find some way to keep his lust for her from taking over. "I think it's for the best."

She sat down on the bar stool and shook her head. "Is it because of our lovely conversation earlier this morning?"

"Thought you'd bring that up." He didn't look at her as he reached for his own mug and took his time refilling. He then returned to his stool.

He needed her to leave, but she'd asked the right question: was it wise for her to go? He had nothing to offer her, no reason to prompt her to stay. "I told Zane about the fortress and the encampments."

"What did he say?"

"Other than expressing his horror with a few well-chosen words, not much. I think we're both in shock. He'll be here in an hour or so. Stone as well. And I've had my communications center get in touch with the rest of the mastyrs, letting them know what's going on."

She nodded, staring at the counter. "Thanks again for being at the gorge, for hunting for me. I know I couldn't have gotten out of there by myself."

He frowned. "I'm still not sure why she didn't make it harder for you to get away."

She met his gaze square on. "I've been thinking the same thing. If she'd really wanted to keep me there, she would have posted guards or something. Or had a patrol on the roof. Or even chained me to the wall. Although …"

"What?"

"I don't know, Ian. Her confidence troubles me. I know I mentioned this last night, but her superior attitude has me worried more than anything else she's done over the past year. Even though she was defeated out at Angler's Cliff, she doesn't seem concerned at all."

He turned the mug in his hands, then tapped his thumb ring against the ceramic. "Your inability to see all the tents in the encampment because of the spell has me worried. I mean, what you've described sounds massive all by itself."

Regan set her cup down and slid off her stool. She walked to the eastern window with a vista leading to the Leberion Plain.

The shutters had already come up, the sun having set on the other side of the house. From the eastern view, she would be able to see the forest on both sides of the gorge.

"I have to go back," she said.

"And you should. You should be with your people." His gaze fell to the shape of her ass, the snug jeans helping him to visualize her naked. He mentally placed a hand on her left cheek. He loved Regan's figure.

She turned, looking at him over her shoulder, and shook her head. "Not to Swanicott. I mean the fortress. I want to fly over there at full-dark and see what the mist tells me. You have to remember, I only saw the mist when I was trying to escape. It wasn't visible from the tower and I need to study it, at least for a few minutes."

"You didn't see the mist when you first arrived?"

"I was unconscious. I woke up in the tower in a lot of pain."

Ian repressed a shudder. He hated the idea that she'd suffered. "Well, there's no way I'm letting you get anywhere near the mist." He set his mug down and rose from his seat at the same time. "I just got you out of the fortress. It would be foolish as hell to be anywhere near that place."

"Temper, Ian." She offered him a taunting smile. She could always set up his back.

He gritted his teeth, grinding his molars. "No way you're going back there."

"Really?" She pivoted in his direction. "Are you forbidding me?"

"Hell, yeah, I am." Once more aware that his vision had been healed, that not even indoor light hurt his eyes any longer, he crossed to her. "This is my realm, in case you've forgotten, and my word is law. You are not returning to the fortress, the mist, the gorge, nowhere. I want you in Swanicott."

She moved within a handful of inches from him. "If I can find a way to help all of you bring that woman down, then I'll do whatever I need to do. I want to help, and for that I need to be close to the spelled mist. Besides, you're not the one who was stuck in Margetta's fortress, who had to endure her torture."

"And you're not the one who sat in the dirt night after night, praying for some kind of opening in the shielding mist so I could find you."

An arrested expression entered her doe eyes. He always forgot how beautiful she was until he stood this close to her. Her skin was like cream, her cheekbones high, and the fae point of her chin softer than most. Her eyes were so warm his heart ached just looking at her. Her sweet jasmine-lime scent rose in a sudden wave, a powerful reminder his life had changed because Regan was a blood rose.

"I wasn't thinking of what you went through," she said in a quiet voice. "Only what needs to be done."

"And what do you think that is?" he asked.

Her brows rose. "To destroy her army, of course."

"So your intention is to swing by, take a look at the mist, hope to hell she or a hundred of her Invictus pairs aren't hanging around looking for you, then head to Swanicott."

"Something like that. Once back at the Fae Guild, I'll start working on a counter-spell. I just need to get a feel for her mist, how she constructed it. And it would help if I was there."

"It's too dangerous right now. My guess is she'll have part of her army out hunting for you tonight as it is."

She caught his arm. "Then take me out there yourself."

"You don't know what you're asking. Margetta will be on guard now. She'll be waiting for you."

But her gaze fell to where her fingers now touched his skin. "You still work out." Her voice had deepened and sounded hoarse.

Desire rose all over again as he remembered how she liked to touch him and do other things. No one had ever pleased him as much as Regan. At the same time, her hand fell away and she shifted to look back out the window. She crossed her arms over her chest. "I shouldn't have touched you. Sweet Goddess, I'm scared."

Nothing she'd said had surprised him more than these words. "You should be afraid of Margetta."

"No, that's not it. I mean, yes I am afraid of the Ancient Fae." She waved a hand between them. "It's you and me. I'm afraid of getting sucked back in." Her eyes widened as she turned back to him. "You hurt me, Ian. You're still hurting me."

"And you've done the same to me."

"I didn't cause the massacre."

"But you might as well have because you enthralled me, the way the powerful fae can do. Your eyes often turned silver when we were together, the way Vojalie's do when she's reading people, entrancing them, taking their minds unaware. You enthralled me, Regan, keeping me by your side when I should have been caring for my people. My sister died and my two nieces. Ben lost his brother. This will always be your fault. You did something to me back then and I'll never forgive you for it."

He moved away from her, all his rage flowing once more in a heavy tornado through his head. He could recall what it had been like that night, flying slowly through Raven's Overlook and seeing blood on every doorstep, children in pieces, several of his Guardsmen decapitated. The funeral pyre had been enormous and burned for two days in order to properly send all the dead to the afterlife.

He'd wept over his sister and her girls. Her husband had been killed as well. His grief had been almost unbearable.

"You're wrong," she countered. "I don't have the ability to enthrall, not like that, and certainly not someone at your power level. I've talked this over with Vojalie and even she doesn't know why my eyes turn silver, but it isn't about enthrallment. You can ask her yourself."

He flared his nostrils, his lips turning down. "So you've become a liar as well."

She moved close to him once more, her fists clenched at her sides, breathing fire at him. Her dark eyes flashed her anger. "Never that, Ian, and you know it."

He knew he was an imposing man, given his mass and his strength. But here she was, the slender fae woman, at least seven inches short than he, and she didn't hesitate to stand up to him. She'd said she was afraid, but he knew she had a lot of natural courage and he respected her for it.

He'd never wanted to believe she was liar, but what other conclusion could he draw? Regan was one of the most powerful fae in the Nine Realms. Known as the Ruby Fae, she'd sat on the Fae Council in Tannisford Realm for at least two centuries before leaving to create the Fae Guild retreat in her home realm of Swanicott.

She was highly respected, not just in the fae community but in all the realm-folk communities of their world. She'd even helped

Mastyr Zane and Olivia defeat a small army of Invictus out at the Dead Zone near Angler's cliff in Swanicott. Regan had dispelled Margetta's non-mist based shield which had kept a massive Invictus camp hidden for decades.

But he'd always believed her accomplishments reflected her guilty conscience, her attempts to atone for her misdeed in keeping him away from Camberlaune at a critical hour. He believed nothing less now.

"Go home to Swanicott, Regan, because I won't allow you to head back up the gorge. Leave the war to the mastyrs."

He turned his back to her, pulled out his cell and contacted Zane. He told Zane to hold off coming to Camberlaune because he was returning Regan to the Swanicott Fae Guild. He also asked him to contact Stone and tell him to wait until Ian was back in Camberlaune before coming to him. The last thing he wanted was a powerful mastyr like Stone getting anywhere near Regan.

~ ~ ~

Regan moved past Ian. In the space of a few minutes, their relationship had reverted to all the old issues. Besides the fact he'd called her a liar, Ian had always thrown his weight around any chance he got.

But she'd been in charge of her own life for a very, very long time. She also had a strong opinion about their current situation. Regan had been a woman of faith from the time she could remember. And in her opinion, the Goddess never did anything without a purpose, including her miraculous escape from the fortress.

Add to that the undeniable fact she'd helped Zane and Olivia demolish the Invictus camp at Angler's Cliff, Regan felt in her bones she was meant to have a role now. But it wouldn't be a bad thing to head back to Swanicott and ask for fae assistance to break the spell. Maybe she could persuade Zane to take her with a large portion of the Swanicott Guard back to Dark Gorge and the mist.

For now, she needed a break from Ian's recriminations.

"Given that Margetta may be in pursuit, I'll fly you home."

"That would probably be best."

"You're not going to fight me anymore?"

"In this case, I think you're right. Margetta might have her army out looking for me and you are a much faster flyer than I am. So, yeah, just take me back to Swanicott."

Regan put on the new leather jacket, then collected the clothes and toiletries Olivia had sent over. She placed them in the striped violet and white satchel they'd come in. When she returned to the foyer, the door was wide open and Ian stood with his back to her. He filled the space from one doorjamb to the other.

At six-six, and built like a tank, he was a big man, very much in Mastyr Jude's mold.

His attention was fixed on the night sky, so she stopped and allowed herself a good long look. Because his arms were bare, she had a stellar view of his ripped, corded muscles. He wore the sleeveless, black leather Guard coat which hung to mid-calf. His long, dark hair, gathered in a woven clasp, hung well down his back. She'd always loved the traditional Guardsman length.

A familiar affection rose up within her before she could stop it and her heart swelled so big she felt like her chest would explode. Damn. She'd always loved him.

And he'd always blamed her.

In a minor way, she'd faulted herself as well or at the very least both of them. They'd been so caught up in their love affair, maybe it had caused Ian to miss critical signs that a major Invictus offensive was on the wind.

The massacre had pulverized them both, ending their affair that very night.

She knew she hadn't done as he'd said; she hadn't enthralled him. But if they hadn't been involved, hadn't loved each other so deeply, would the massacre have ever happened? Would Ian have seen the signs in his realm? Had his love for her and his drive toward her prevented him from being a proper ruler of his realm?

Maybe what hurt most, however, was he truly believed her capable of such horrendous wrong-doing. Although, she suspected he'd been using her as a scapegoat to salve his own feelings of guilt. Yet, Ian hadn't done anything wrong; he'd just loved her.

But she couldn't change the past or his beliefs.

She lifted her chin. "I'm ready to go."

Ian turned in her direction and held out his arm to her. He was a quick flyer and despite the ocean between the realms, he'd have her home in no time.

She crossed the foyer and went outside with him, savoring for a brief moment the feel of his hand on the small of her back. He even took her satchel from her. "I'll carry it."

As she climbed aboard his foot, he pathed softly, *Regan.* Just her name, but she was always surprised by the way his voice sounded so deep and supremely sexy even within her mind.

Yes? She responded. *Did you forget something?*

When he slid his arm around her waist, it was all she could do to keep from crying out. It was like being held in the most beautiful embrace, even though it was just a simple flight hold.

Apologies. I shouldn't have yelled at you.

Which part exactly? She had to ask the question. She didn't want any misunderstandings.

For saying what didn't need to be repeated. You know what I believe, but I didn't mean to distress you.

You didn't. You made me furious then really sad that you hold such a wretched opinion of me. No, please don't say anything more. Just take me home.

She slid her arm around his neck, but set her face forward.

She was done.

She mentally started making plans. As soon as Ian had her safely back at the Fae Guild retreat, she would contact the Fae Council in Tannisford and make a case for the most powerful fae to work with her to eradicate Margetta's mist-spell. She'd seen enough before her escape to know it was much more complex than the spell that had hidden the Invictus camp near Angler's Cliff.

She felt Ian's muscles shift in a way that meant he was ready to levitate and take off flying. Then, he stopped, his body growing oddly stiff.

"Shit. Stone's here. Zane must not have reached him in time."

Stone, Mastyr of Tannisford Realm, dropped down in front of them, fifteen feet distant. He was taller than Ian, almost six-seven, had thick, wavy, black hair, unusual green eyes, and more tats than even Ian. His appearance had always reminded Regan of a hawk, the way his eyes focused like a predator on whatever he was looking at.

Her heart picked up its cadence. She blinked a couple of times because Stone had never looked more handsome in his life, though she couldn't say why. A sudden and very powerful desire began to rise within her. She'd always liked and admired Stone, but she'd never experienced a romantic interest in him like she did now.

She also felt his chronic blood starvation like a pressure against her breastbone. She wanted to feed him. Needed to. And she needed to do it now.

At about the same time, she felt something very strange flow through Ian, a vibration unfamiliar to Regan. The muscles of his back flexed and released only to tighten again.

A strange chuffing sound came out of his throat. She looked up at him, shocked to see that his fangs had settled low on his lips. "Ian?"

A low growl came from his throat as he slowly slid his arm from around her then eased her away from him. At the last moment, he pushed her behind him.

"Get in the house. Now." His voice was low, almost unrecognizable.

Regan didn't understand until she heard Stone growl as well. He stared at her, a hungry glint in his eye, nostrils flared, fangs on his lips.

Oh, no.

It was all so new she'd forgotten: *she was a blood rose.* And Stone was one of the most powerful of all the ruling mastyrs.

Her heart set up a heavy racket, the pulse sounding in her ears. The blood rose part of her felt ramped up and excited beyond words for what was about to happen. The other part, the sensible, womanly fae part knew these men were in deep trouble since each had quickly devolved into a primordial state.

She trembled from both excitement and horror. She needed to do something, yet she was unable to move; she wanted to see the men fight for her.

Ian charged first, levitating and flying at Stone so fast he was only a blur. Using his head, he caught Stone in the chest, forcing him backward several yards. He landed on top of Stone at the foot of a large boulder not eight feet from the cliff edge.

When Ian rose up, Stone flew upward with a combination of levitation and sheer strength, catching Ian's chin with his fist.

As Ian's head jerked back, he flew in an arc through the air, then came to earth with a dull thud, landing on his back not far from where she stood. But by the time Stone moved in again, Ian was already on his feet and the battle was on.

Fists flew, the men grunted when struck and at times howled with a kind of fury Regan had never heard before.

They were equally matched and as they struck each other, they neared the cliff edge. Regan's excitement began to wear off, replaced by an almost paralyzing dread.

She began to shake as the nature of the battle settled in hard. This would be a fight to the death over possession of her.

And she couldn't let it happen. She couldn't be the cause of the Nine Realms losing one of their most powerful mastyrs at a time when their world was on the brink of a civilization-ending war.

She sank to her knees.

She had to look away from the battling pair and close her ears to their terrible guttural sounds.

She had to reach Vojalie and she had to do it now.

There was one thing she did understand about her blood rose state. All the women who for whatever reason launched into this new state of being also gained power.

She took deep breaths and let her blood rose ability add new strength to her telepathic skill. The resulting vibration stunned her, but she made quick work and summoned the one woman who could help her.

Vojalie, she pathed. *I'm in trouble. Please hear me. Vojalie, I learned early this morning I'm a blood rose and right now Mastyrs Stone and Ian are battling, but neither is in possession of a rational mind. They will fight to the death if something isn't done. Can you help me?*

For a moment, nothing returned, but it wasn't Vojalie who responded. Instead Davido, her husband, a very ancient and powerful troll, pathed, *We'll be with you in a matter of seconds. Stay out of harm's way and we'll join you at your location.*

Thank the Goddess, was all she could think to respond.

Tears streaked down her cheeks as she rose to her feet, her knees shaking. She stayed put, hating the sounds of the men roaring at each other, these men who had always been such excellent friends. Each had blood pouring off his body and so many bruises.

They were within two feet of the cliff edge. Regan shouted, "Ian. Stone. Look where you are!" If either tumbled off without engaging their levitation skills, they could hit the cliff wall and be knocked unconscious. With five hundred feet to go, serious injury and possibly death could follow.

But she might as well have whispered for all the good it did.

The next moment, she felt the arrival of Vojalie and Davido. She turned to them. "I'm so grateful you've come. I didn't know what else to do. I can't stop them."

"Perfectly understandable," Davido said. No one knew his exact age, only that he'd lived a very long time and was as wise as he was old. He also had a tremendous amount of power.

And as the two men took their battle over the cliff, Davido levitated a few feet off the ground, something most trolls couldn't do. He then headed after them and disappeared into the gorge as well.

Regan put a hand to her chest. Anything could happen in a situation like this.

Don't worry, the powerful fae pathed. *Davido will take care of this. You'll see.*

Regan began counting her breaths. She wanted to go to the edge of the cliff to see what had happened, but couldn't make her feet move.

The next moment, all three men returned, levitating above the edge of the gorge, Davido between and holding each by the arm.

Both Ian and Stone appeared confused as though they didn't know what had happened.

Vojalie urged Regan to return to the house with her. "Let the men figure this out first."

"Absolutely."

Now that the terrifying situation had been brought to an end, Regan shook worse than ever. Her legs felt rubbery as she made her way back into the foyer.

It looked like her plan to return to Swanicott wouldn't be as simple as she'd imagined. There were other mastyr vampires in each of the realms. If she left Ian's side and one of them came after her, she knew by the strength of her reaction to Stone, she wouldn't be able to resist bonding with the first one to gain her attention.

Better to stick close to the devil she knew, especially since Ian would resist completing the blood rose bond with her. In that sense, she could buy a lot of time here in Camberlaune.

Anywhere else, she'd be at risk.

Chapter Three

A few minutes later, with Regan safely ensconced in his library, Ian sat opposite Stone in his living room. Stone held an ice pack to his face and kept moving his jaw back and forth. He sat on an ottoman, his body angled forward with one elbow supported on his thigh.

Ian leaned back on the sofa, a pack of frozen peas pressed to the bridge of his nose. Stone had gotten in several major hits, but this one had practically slammed his nose into his brain. Davido had done him a solid and set the bone.

Oh, shit had it hurt.

Davido's blue eyes glittered as he glanced from one man to the other. "Sorry I missed the first part of the brawl. Must have been a sight to see." He rubbed his hands together.

Stone glanced at Ian, and offered a crooked smile. His lip was bleeding. "It was a sight to *hurt,* I'll say that."

Ian chuckled. "It was."

"And Ian, those rings of yours … *brutal.*"

"What were we thinking?"

At that, a shard of concern passed through Stone's swollen eyes. "I didn't think. I saw Regan and I was done for. Why didn't you warn me she was a blood rose?"

"Zane was supposed to head you off. Didn't he call?"

Stone shook his head. "My phone rang, but I was already in flight. And he might have tried pathing, but lately my telepathic frequency has been hit-and-miss."

Ian nodded. "It happens."

Stone narrowed his eyes. "But were you actually going to let her out of your sight?"

Ian shook his head, shifting his gaze to the floor, working to think it all through. "I don't know what to tell you. I knew what the other mastyrs had said on the loop. Guess I hadn't thought it out, or not as far as I needed to."

Davido brought him a scotch neat. Ian drank it quickly, but came up sputtering. Even his throat felt swollen from the fight.

Finally, he answered Stone's question. "It was all too new and we'd been quarreling as we do when we spend more than a few minutes in each other's company. I needed her to leave and she wanted to go." He shook his head several times. "I can't believe I was going to take her to Swanicott and leave her there."

The horror of what he'd almost done and how he would have essentially left her wide open to other mastyrs, made every bruise on his body throb. His nose started bleeding again.

Davido brought him a couple of tissues and refilled his tumbler.

Ian plugged up both nostrils. He then leaned his head onto the cushion, removed the bag of peas and pinched the bridge of his nose. After a minute, he gently pushed the tissue aside and slowly sipped the scotch. The burn did him some good.

He'd engaged his healing power, most of it focused on his smashed nose. But sweet Goddess, he hurt in so many places, he was afraid to move.

"So, tell me about the fortress," Stone said.

Ian related everything Regan had told him, adding that because of the mist, he'd only seen a small portion of one of the south-facing stone walls. "But the army size, according to Regan, would indicate we would need to join forces to accomplish much of anything."

Stone nodded, shifting his ice pack to his opposite cheek. Davido offered him a tumbler as well and Stone took it, throwing it back, then wincing. "Shouldn't have done that. Ian, what the hell did you do to my neck?"

Ian could only laugh, but he groaned afterward since his ribs ached. "Not sure. But if it makes you feel any better, I think you broke a couple of my ribs."

"No, it doesn't help at all." But Stone smiled as he slowly blew air from his cheeks then took another gulp of whisky.

Ian's thoughts took a turn as he considered Regan's blood rose state. How naïve he'd been, or maybe just ignorant, to think he could drop her off in Swanicott and not think twice about it.

But even these few thoughts brought his fangs descending. He knew there were several lesser mastyr vampires in Swanicott who would have been equally drawn to Regan as either he or Stone were.

A growl escaped his throat before he could prevent it.

"So," Davido drawled. "What's going on now? Are you planning to attack Mastyr Stone again? Do I need to prepare myself to intervene once more?"

Ian glanced at Davido, wondering what the hell he was talking about, then came to a sudden awareness of his fang-state. He covered his mouth with his hand. "Shit, sorry. I was thinking about what could have happened if I'd actually taken Regan back to her realm." He worked at retracting his fangs.

Davido stared at him, his blue eyes twinkling with amusement.

He was one of the ugliest trolls Ian had ever known. His skin was heavily wrinkled, and his three forehead ridge rolls sprouted hair in a few places.

Despite his lack of looks, women flocked to the short man because of his abundant charisma. That he'd wooed and won the beautiful Vojalie spoke to his nature more than anything else. He was a good man, an excellent father, and made a strong habit of not taking life too seriously. In fact, all he did at present was serve two mastyr vampires a healthy dose of scotch; he didn't even dispense advice.

"What am I supposed to do, Davido? You know my history with Regan."

The three rolls of Davido's forehead squinched up. "Now, how am I supposed to have an answer to such a question? I'm not a vampire for one thing nor do I have the smallest idea what it feels like to suddenly be obsessed with a blood rose. Sorry, my boy, but I can't help you at all." He jerked his thumb in Stone's direction. "Though you might want to think about sending this one packing."

Ian met Stone's amused gaze. "That was my first thought, but we need him here. How about you spend the night's rotation with Ben until I get things with Regan figured out? My instincts tell me I'm going to need your battling support."

Stone nodded, holding his tumbler out to Davido who in turn added another two fingers. "I agree. Besides, it seems to me we might have a chance to end this war for good now that we know where Margetta's fortress is."

Ian ran a hand through his hair. Somewhere in the battling, he'd lost his woven Guardsman's clasp. Stone had as well.

A thought occurred to him. "Hold on. Malik said he did something to keep Zane from chasing Willow, but what was that?"

"I remember now," Stone said. "It was all over the loop. Malik took some of Willow's blood and spread it up his forearms in long streaks. Zane said it worked, that his obsessive drive toward Willow ended abruptly."

"That's what we'll do, then."

Davido cleared his throat.

Ian frowned at him. "What?"

"Won't you need to ask Regan if she's on board?"

"I don't see her compliance as an issue."

Davido shook his head. "You were always absurdly stubborn. But let us hope she's as willing to oblige you as you think she is. You haven't exactly given her reason to adore your sweet self."

Ian's lips quirked. "That last bit is very true, but Regan has a sensible side." At least he hoped she'd be practical given their current predicament.

~ ~ ~

Regan sat on the black leather couch in the library. "I forgot what it was like with Ian on every front, the good parts and the bad. From the time I fed him at the bottom of the gorge, I've felt as though I've gotten stuck on a carnival ride with way too many sudden highs and lows. I'm ready to get off, as in now."

Vojalie nodded several times in succession. "Are you still determined to return to Swanicott?"

"I want to make use of the significant resources at my fae retreat, and I intend to contact the Fae Council. It's time we, as a fae community, stepped up together to confront Margetta. Surely, as a working unit we can uncover a spell to rid her encampment of the shielding mist."

"Did you try to solve the spell while you were there?"

Regan thought back to the sequence of events since she didn't see the wall of mist until she'd escaped from the tower. "Though I was able to detect a spell over a portion of the camp tents, the best I could do was to imprint the spell in my mind. I had no luck, however, dissecting the formula at all. And you have no idea how hard I tried. I think there might have been a blocking spell in place.

"As far as the mist goes, its presence came as a huge surprise. I'd had no idea there was even a spell along the southern edge of the property until I'd reached the catwalk. By then, I had very little time to escape. So, no, I was never near the mist long enough to take a reasonable stab at its composition."

Vojalie's brow grew pinched as though she was mulling the situation over. She sat in a leather, wing-back chair, and was somewhat swallowed up because it was built on Ian's massive lines. Her right wrist dangled just over the armrest. With her free hand, she twirled a long, dark curl around her finger.

Regan kept expecting Vojalie to respond to her observation but she remained silent. She almost looked perplexed.

"What is it?" Regan asked. "Don't you think my idea has merit? That we should involve the fae community?"

Vojalie huffed a small, almost frustrated sigh. "In some respects yes, though I have my reservations. But only you can determine the right path for yourself and for Ian."

"Do you have a better idea?"

"Actually, I don't. I've never excelled at spell-making, so I'm of no use to you in this situation. But I have been close to several of the blood roses over the past few months. And I've observed that each one eventually had to alter her thinking in order to move forward, especially where the realm mastyr was concerned." She looked almost pained, her hands now clasped tightly together, as she added, "If at all possible, make every effort to see Ian in a new light."

"I don't know what you mean."

Vojalie appeared to hunt for words. "You don't know him very well, Regan. We could start there."

"You're so wrong," Regan answered quickly. "I know him extremely well. You forget, we were lovers once."

Vojalie shook her head. "I'm sorry, but I strongly disagree. You were enamored of him many centuries ago, you had a terrible falling out, and you've barely exchanged an hour of conversation since. How can you possibly say you know him well? I would suggest, you don't know him at all."

Regan wanted to argue, but something in what Vojalie said struck a chord of truth within Regan's fae nature. "Part of me wishes to argue the point, but maybe you're right. In some ways, we were just getting to know each other, even to have the occasional argument, when Raven's Overlook changed everything."

Vojalie had been her mentor from the time she was a teenage girl nearly seven centuries ago. Regan had lived a long time and in turn had mentored dozens of fae women herself.

What she had never done well, however, was enjoy a long-term relationship with a man. She'd dated dozens of times since

Ian, but most of her affairs only lasted a brief couple of years. After all this time, she wasn't sure she'd ever have a real relationship.

Shifting her thoughts for a moment, she considered the lightning-and-thunder nature of her brief love affair with Ian. Was it possible she'd been part of the problem as Ian suggested, even if she'd never quite seen it before? Not the 'enthralling' part; Regan knew she'd hadn't put Ian in any kind of trance. Yet, how many times had she begged Ian to stay with her just a few more minutes, sometimes extending his visit by an hour or two.

If she had guilt, it lay there. Maybe by letting him go sooner the night of the massacre, he might have been able to save his people.

"When I'm with a man, I'm all in, but the relationships never seem to last. With Ian, I'd always seduce him to stay longer with me than he should. It was wrong."

"So you do blame yourself."

"How could I not feel guilty because of what happened? Maybe if Ian had been there at the time, he could have prevented the massacre. However, that's something we'll never know. But I promise you, I didn't enthrall him. My only excuse can be that I was out-of-my-mind in love with him."

Vojalie leaned back in her chair. "Well, you definitely have a complicated relationship with Ian. But I would strongly encourage you to stick close to him at least for the next few nights. I know this is all new to you, but Stone's reaction will be the first of many. And once it's known you're a blood rose, there are some mastyrs, anxious for more power, who will do whatever they can to trap you into a bond. Are you aware this is a possibility?"

Regan nodded. "I believe that's what happened to Samantha. A mastyr named Ry was after her and almost succeeded in forcing a bond."

"Yes, he did. And he was also aligned with Margetta. So, I urge you to keep these difficult facts in front of you as a reminder how serious this situation is, especially for you."

Regan knew Vojalie was right. "I'll do as you've said. My earliest thoughts were more a primal reaction, to put as much distance between myself and Ian as I could."

She heard footsteps down the hall and a moment later, Ian appeared in the doorway. His bruises looked better. He had a concerned frown between his brows as he met her gaze. "Thought we should talk."

She nodded. "We should." She rose from the sofa and crossed to him.

To Vojalie, Ian said, "Your husband is pouring out two glasses of a very fine cognac for you both. He said he refuses to return to Merhaine until you've had a drink with him. Shall I send him in?"

Vojalie rolled her eyes. "That man. He takes every opportunity to flirt."

"You are so right, my dearest love." Carrying a brandy snifter in each hand, Davido pushed past Ian. "You will love this, my most darling sweetheart. The very finest brandy. Ian said he's been keeping it just for us."

Regan watched the couple for a moment. They'd been together a long time, but Davido still treated his woman as though they were dating. She'd always admired them as a couple.

When Davido handed the snifter to his wife, she leaned forward and tilted her face to him. Davido caught her chin with his now free hand and Regan could sense a brief telepathic exchange. He then kissed Vojalie and sat down in the companion wing-back chair. He was only five-three and his feet didn't hit the floor, not in a chair designed for Guard-sized bodies.

But was anyone as comfortable in his skin as Davido, or Vojalie for that matter?

"Regan?" Ian drew her attention away from the couple now clinking glasses and smiling tenderly at each other.

As she turned and moved into the hall, he closed the door to the library. In a low voice, he murmured, "Thought we should give them some alone time."

"Right." She glanced up at him, nervous suddenly. "Ian, Vojalie thinks I should stay here, with you."

He looked down at her, scowling. "Not sure we have much of a choice given the situation. Stone left. I sent him to Ben at the Communication Center."

"But you don't want me here."

"I don't want a lot of things. I don't *want* that Margetta abducted you from your home or held you for a month, or that you're a blood rose. And I definitely wish I hadn't battled Stone because I'm beat up as all hell. But Stone did make a suggestion and I think we should do it."

He led her into the living room but didn't gesture for her to sit. Instead, he stood facing her, his ringed fingers gathered into fists and planted on his hips. He'd taken off his Guard coat but now wore a black tank, exposing a large part of the broad tattoo that covered his chest and parts of his arms and shoulders. The figure of a hawk in flight hadn't existed when they'd dated.

But it did now.

Her breathing hitched. She'd always felt this way around Ian, like she could stumble and fall so easily and in more ways than one.

She dragged her attention away from his chest and back to his eyes. This was unfortunate because his nostrils flared after which his eyes dropped to half-mast. "See something you want?" His deep forest-fern scent flowed over her in heavy waves.

She drew close and grabbed his tank t-shirt with one hand and pulled it into a knot. "Always. And that's a big part of this problem. You shouldn't be built like every woman's darkest fantasy."

He slid his hands over her hips then down her bottom, squeezing. "Is that what I am to you? A dark fantasy?"

"Yeah, except this isn't a fantasy, is it? This is you, in the flesh, in front of me."

Though she could feel his resistance, he leaned down and captured her lips with his own.

Heat, then fire.

Pressure, then a demanding tongue.

She released his shirt to slide her arm around his neck. He used his hands on her bottom to press her against him, no doubt so she could feel the hard length of him, feel what she'd missed all this time.

Ian, she pathed.

Regan, came back to her, a low resonance through her mind. *I've missed you, missed this.*

I know. Me, too.

He drew back and settled his forehead against hers. He was breathing hard. She was no different.

A rhythmic thumping came from the direction of the library. Regan pulled away from Ian, her eyes wide. She felt a blush climb her cheeks. "Is that what I think it is?" she whispered.

"Yeah. The troll is getting it on—"

Regan finished the sentence. "With his wife."

"Yup."

"How do they do it? Did you see how he is with her? He should write a book on how to love a woman."

"I'd read it. Your gender is mostly a mystery to me, to most men."

A high-pitched squeal forced Regan's hands to her lips and when a trollish groan followed, Ian shook his head, laughing softly.

"What do we do now?" Regan asked.

"I don't know. Wait till they come out, I guess."

Regan chuckled. "I didn't mean about Vojalie and Davido. I meant about us."

He turned back to her, frowning. "You need to stay here in Camberlaune. It was stupid to think I could let you take off. I'd be worried about you the whole time because if some other mastyr ever got hold of you, some bastard without a conscience, you could end up in a bonded relationship that could hurt you forever. And I don't think I'd be able to forgive myself. Maybe I have issues with what happened a long time ago, but I don't have a problem with you sticking close, not until all of this is settled.

"Besides, you know the lay-out of Margetta's fortress and encampment. None of the rest of us do. You're the logical person to answer all the questions any of us will have.

"And Stone reminded me about something Mastyr Malik had shared with us. When he was battling the Invictus in his realm, he'd asked Zane to come in for support. When Zane reacted to Willow in the same way Stone recently responded to you, Malik used a small portion of Willow's blood and painted streaks up both arms. Zane said it made a huge difference in his ability to withstand the pull toward Willow."

"That's right," Regan said. "I remember hearing something about that."

Ian offered a half-smile. "I have no doubt Malik made sure Zane stayed away from Willow, but it really helped. What do you say? Will you mark me with your blood?"

Regan knew she'd just stumbled into really dangerous territory. Everything about the situation warned her to keep her distance but here he was suggesting she mark him to help keep other mastyrs away. It was bad enough she'd already agreed to stick close to him until they had everything figured out. But the giving of her blood in such an earthy cavewoman sort of way, had warning bells clanging loudly inside her head.

"Ian, is it really necessary? Can't we just make sure that I'm not around other unbonded mastyrs?"

He might have answered, but Davido called to him. Regan shifted to look past Ian and saw that Vojalie stood beside her man. The troll was grinning ear to ear and a warm blush suffused his wife's face.

Vojalie held his arm, her eyes full of affection as she looked down at him.

Davido called out. "We must be going, Ian. Thank you for the cognac." His smile broadened when he looked at Regan. "And I suggest you indulge your interest in the mastyr. Life is very short, even for us long-lived types. Make the most of every opportunity."

And with the extraordinary power the troll possessed, the couple simply vanished.

"With so much ability between them," Regan said, "why don't they battle alongside us?"

"I've wondered the same thing, and I've asked Davido to intervene with Margetta, but he refuses. He said he made war for the first thousand years of his life, but promised himself never again. I guess if you've served that long as a warrior, it's enough, no matter how many centuries you added to your belt after."

He glanced behind him. "Listen, are you hungry? My housekeeper always keeps soup and some of her homemade bread stocked in my refrigerator."

At the suggestion, she put a hand to her stomach. "I'm starved, so yes, I'd love some."

He gestured with his hand for her to precede him. She led the way across the foyer to his great room, an open area of his house encompassing a north view of the mountains.

He directed her to sit at the island bar, where earlier he'd served her coffee, then moved easily from the pots and pans, to the fridge, and back. He was comfortable in the kitchen and Regan couldn't help but smile. Ian had been a bachelor a long time, but when she'd dated him, he wouldn't have spent a second building a fire and setting up the spit to roast some meat. He'd had staff back then to take care of him and he'd made use of them.

Though he had a housekeeper now, apparently he no longer minded doing some of the cooking.

"Did you make the coffee, too?"

"Sure." He chuckled softly. "I know what you're thinking. I remember how you went into the woods yourself so long ago and collected firewood. It pissed you off that I ordered my servants to the task."

She smiled. "I was perfectly capable of scouring your land for some deadfall. And so were you."

"You even started bringing your axe to my house." The vegetable beef soup was heating in a pot on the stove and already smelled heavenly. Ian leaned on the island marble, his smile warm as he held her gaze.

"I'm a resourceful person," she said, "though I will confess it's much easier now with food grown in bulk and shipped to markets, with electricity and how about the microwave?"

Ian grinned. "One of my favorite things. That and cell phones. I mean, not everyone can communicate telepathically and I can reach any of my Guardsmen at any time. What did we do without all our gadgets?"

She shrugged but smiled. "We headed into the forest. Do you remember the time you brought down a buck?"

"Of course. Used my bow and arrow."

"You shared it with the village, too, the one at the base of the Rim near the Peralin River. Pikon, I think, at least that's what I remember. You know, I swear that's when I fell in love with you."

His brows rose. "Because I gave away venison I'd never be able to use?"

"You could have dried it. You didn't have to share."

He sighed, his gaze shifting past her but not appearing to land on anything particular. "I suppose, but it was a rough winter that year and some of the families had it hard. How could I not have shared? What kind of mastyr would that have made me?"

He turned back to his soup and using a wooden spoon, stirred slowly. He already had thick slices of bread all buttered and toasting in the oven.

Her gaze became fixed to the back of his head. Vojalie wasn't entirely right that Regan didn't know Ian. She knew he was generous and self-sacrificing as most vampire Guardsmen were.

Her heart got that swollen feeling again. She leaned her elbow on the cool marble, and dropped her chin into her hand. She had to repress a heavy sigh. She was close to mooning after the man all over again.

"I'll do it, Ian, the protective blood streaks. I think it's the smart thing to do. Maybe I can't be bound to you right now, but I know we'll be better off if we follow Mastyr Malik's lead."

Afterward stacking up the toasted sour dough on a plate, he ladled soup into two bowls. He met her gaze. "That means a lot to me."

She wished he wasn't so damn handsome. Just looking at him sent desire skyrocketing.

He brought a bowl around for her as well as a spoon and napkin. "Dig in," he said. "I have a feeling this is going to be a long night."

~ ~ ~

Ian could hardly taste the soup. For some reason, the jasmine-lime scent Regan carried as a blood rose had invaded the kitchen, though he didn't know why. The problem was his cock loved it, couldn't get enough, and wouldn't settle down especially knowing she'd be opening a vein soon to create the protective streaks on his arms. He almost groaned at the thought.

He dipped his spoon in the soup but didn't dare look at Regan. And it didn't help at all that she kept making her cooing sounds because she was enjoying her food. She might have a well-developed spiritual side and spent most of her time teaching in her fae retreat, but she was also extremely sensual.

She loved life, loved good food, and she adored sex.

He took a big bite of sour dough bread, hoping the flavors would mitigate her exquisite scent.

No such luck.

"You okay?" she asked.

"Not even a little."

She chuckled. "This soup is to die for. My compliments to your housekeeper. And the bread, well, what can I say ... heaven."

"She'll appreciate your compliments."

When the meal was over, he did a quick clean-up of dishes. Regan brought the empty bowls, plates and spoons to him, but remained very quiet.

Glancing at her, he thought he understood why because he was feeling the same thing. He'd be piercing her vein soon and given the reality she was a blood rose, besides her seductive scent and their past history, sharp desire ran through him.

The heightened color on her cheeks as well as her flowery-lime scent spoke its own tale.

By the time he hung up his dish towel, he felt like a kid on a first date.

He caught her hand in his. "How about we get this over with before one of us explodes."

She giggled. "I feel ridiculous, Ian, like I'm sixteen. I'm so nervous and we're not even doing anything."

He leaned close and spoke against her ear. "No, I'm just going to pierce the veins of your wrist. That's all." He rubbed his nose against her cheek, then pressed his lips to hers very gently.

When she pulled back, he stared into glimmering, doe eyes. "Where do you want to do this?" she asked.

"Out on the walkway if you're game. I want to feel the fresh air flowing off the mountain."

"Sounds wonderful."

They had this in common, a love of the outdoors. Civilized life had a lot to offer, no question about that. But give him a full night spent in one of the Nine Realms' many beautiful forests, and he was a happy man.

Of course, the last time he'd hiked for a few hours with Regan had been one of the happiest of his life. The rest, all which had happened at Raven's Overlook, he wouldn't think about right now.

Instead, he took her hand and led her through the living room to the sliding glass door and out onto the walkway overlooking Dark Gorge.

The air was fresh and cool, even chilly. But he felt hot from stem to stern and he knew it was because of Regan. His drive toward her had his sex ramped up, no question about that. Yet, this felt like more, like a new kind of power had begun to flow through him, a steady vibration of energy and heat, making him glad he wore only the tank right now, and not the Guard coat. He was warm enough as it was with the leather pants and thigh boots. The cool winter air helped as well.

Even Regan didn't seem cold as she leaned against the sturdy wood railing and settled her gaze on the forested cliff opposite. It was early December now, not quite winter, but his elevation was low enough he rarely saw snow at his cliffside home. But the mountains were capped permanently now at least until mid-March, even April, depending on how cold the season would prove to be.

He moved next to her, then gently took her wrist in hand.

She met his gaze, hers as direct as ever. "You can feed as well if you need sustenance. You know I'm willing."

He nodded, but his chest tightened as he looked down at her. What he really wanted to do was take the vein at her throat. But the thought of drinking from her neck hardened an already stiff arousal. At least the leathers kept him snug and not too exposed, but he had it bad.

He caught her chin and kissed her again, another soft touch of his lips to hers. "Thank you. And I'll take you up on your offer."

She shifted to make reaching her wrist a simple thing. He lifted her slender arm until he had the right angle above the collection of veins at the base of her palm. His fangs descended and his breathing took another difficult turn. He couldn't remember the last time he'd been this worked up before a bite.

He didn't strike, yet. Instead, he took a long look at the night sky in a complete three-sixty to make sure there were no Invictus around.

Seeing nothing to mar the view of the stars, he reverted his attention to her arm. Taking a deep breath, he lowered his head and with a helluva lot of practice, struck to the right depth. Forming a seal over the punctures, he began to suck.

But the long groan that left Regan's mouth did little to mitigate his other growing problem.

Chapter Four

Regan had fed plenty of vampires over the course of her centuries of living. And she'd fed Ian when they'd dated. But it had never been like this.

A soft vibration flowed over her entire body, full of desire and latent with power. More than at any other time in the past twenty-four hours, she felt in her bones she was a blood rose. Her destiny had come to her, maybe because of Ian, to provide a mastyr with blood rich enough to end forever his chronic blood starvation.

She was essentially a woman of service, so even if she hadn't cared about Ian as much as she already did, she would have felt grateful to be able to help out.

Thank you, Regan. He lifted his gaze to her, his nostrils working like bellows as he continued to drink from her.

She smiled. "You're welcome. It means a lot to me that I've taken away your pain."

He suckled for another minute, then eased away from her wrist, though he didn't seal the wounds. He was about to use his finger to paint the lines on his skin, from his wrist to his elbow, when she stopped him.

"Allow me." The vibration grew stronger. "Can you feel that?"

He still held her arm in a gentle clasp. His color was heightened despite the chilly air on the deck. "I can. What the hell is this between us, Regan?"

She shook her head. "I don't know. But I want you to seal the wrist wound. I think I need to do something else here."

"You sure?"

"Yes. Absolutely."

Using his tongue, he swiped over the two punctures on her wrist and the small incisions faded to nothing. "What do you have in mind?"

She offered the index finger of her right hand. "Bite me here."

His eyes rolled in his head at her not-so-subtle command. His scent sharpened and she loved it, loved he was so into her. She planted her left hand on his bare shoulder. "I need to create the marks, so make it good."

"It'll hurt."

"I know, but I need a steady stream for this."

His fangs descended once more and with a quick jab, he sliced open her finger. The sudden strike made her gasp, but she ignored the pain of the cut.

She slid her left hand down his arm and using her right forefinger, painted a slow line down the center of his forearm all the way to his wrist bone. Without Ian's tongue to stop the bleeding, the cut flowed freely.

"Take some of this," she said. "I want this to be right." She held her forefinger up for him and he took it in his mouth, sucking once more. She didn't stop him right away because she loved the look on his face, his eyes at half-mast, pupils dilated.

I need you, Regan.

She thought a clear intent would be best. *I'm with you all the way.*

He groaned softly. *Tell me what to do. Is this enough of a mark?*

She shook her head. "I'll be making three on each arm, but I want to stop in between in order to keep the lines clean."

She still held his arm as he nodded, then relinquished her finger. The blood flowed better because he'd suckled. As a vampire, he released chemicals when he drank to keep the body from healing the fang-wound until he was done.

She began the second mark, moving slowly down his arm. The line formed a slight angle to the original one. Once the line was complete, she stopped just as she'd said she would and had him suckle again. Each time, he got a hungry look in his eye which fed her own growing desire to be with him.

After a moment, she created the third line. When she was finished with his right arm, she repeated the process with his left.

When she was done, the same strange vibration flowed from her hand stronger than ever.

He stared at his arm. "I don't recognize this vibration, Regan, do you?"

"No. It's not familiar at all. But look at the lines. Sweet Goddess, what's happening?"

Regan pulled his arm forward and peered at the stripes of blood. She'd expected them to melt, instead, they were transforming, shaping themselves into deep burgundy lines. "They look like tattoos."

She had no idea if they were permanent or not, but her heart beat hard in her chest at the sight of them.

He caught her gaze. "You've marked me, Regan. Yet, somehow this has become more than just a simple warning to other mastyrs. And you're dripping again."

"What?"

He caught her finger in his hand and took it in his mouth.

"Oh," she murmured softly. He needed to seal up the wound.

She felt knocked sideways by all of it, by the feel of the vibrations flowing between them yet centered on his arms, by the way he suckled, and because his forest-fern scent flowed over her now in heavy waves.

She felt his tongue touch the slice on her finger and the next moment, her skin knit together. She was relieved to have the sting gone, but at the same time, wished he would continue. She'd always loved it when Ian drank from her.

With the small wound sealed, he surprised her by pulling her into his arms and kissing her. And not a gentle pressure this time, but an invasion.

Sweet Goddess, how she loved his arms around her and his tongue in her mouth pulsing. For a good, long moment, she forgot everything, forgot the difficulties between them or that their enemy had a fortress in Camberlaune, no doubt preparing for invasion.

Instead, she allowed herself to savor Ian, the strength of his body, the sensual feel of his kiss, and his forest scent.

She could feel the markings on his arms as well, like another pair of arms, surrounding her, protecting her. But even as she experienced these things, she knew the marking bond wasn't complete.

She drew back, holding onto both of his forearms. "We need to do something else."

"Yes, we do." He dipped down and tried to kiss her again, but she put a hand on his chest, chuckling softly. "Not that. I mean, yes, I want to be with you, but the marking bond isn't complete."

"What do you mean? It feels perfect."

"Yes, it is. For you. But every fae sense I have tells me I need to do something else, something more." She thought for a moment then she understood. "Oh, I see. Ian, you have to mark my arms in the same way I've marked yours, only using your blood this time. This will strengthen the shared vibration."

He met her gaze. "I wish I understood what was happening here. Do you get this? The purpose of it?"

"Not all of it, though it feels very protective in nature. But I do sense the marks will increase each of our abilities, though in what way I have no idea."

He nodded. "I would agree with your take on it because this vibration feels full of power."

"Are you concerned about marking me in return? Does this feel like it will be too much of a connection between us?"

He slid his gaze away from her, no doubt exploring the vibration himself. Finally, he shook his head, reverting his gaze to her. His eyes narrowed. "I don't have a sense this is about a bond, more like power we'll be able to use."

"I agree." She then held out her arms to him and smiled. "Just do me, Ian."

He held her gaze steadily and when a new wave of his earthy, erotic scent rolled over her, he added fuel to the fire by throwing a growl into the mix. Once more, his fangs emerged. Only this time he punctured the tip of his right index finger and began creating the trails as she had, first with a center line almost from the elbow of her right arm, all the way to the wrist bone, followed by angled lines down each side.

When he was done, he took both her hands in his, frowning. She understood why. The power she'd been feeling had doubled on them both. The vibrations raced up her arms and down her back, flowing from her hands and into his, then returning the journey.

"Holy shit." He held on, his frown deepening. "Regan, what's going here? Is this because you're a blood rose?"

"I think so. And because you're a very powerful mastyr vampire." She thought it was an idea worth exploring, but his cell phone rang and he instinctively let go of her hands to retrieve it. With their physical connection broken, the vibrations drifted away as swiftly as they'd come.

"Hey, Ben," he said, his cell to his ear. "Everything's good here. I have Regan with me and I'll be sticking close for a while, especially since she's seen Margetta's fortress and her army."

He paused to listen to whatever Ben was saying.

Regan moved away, needing a moment to think. Whatever this was between them, it was happening fast and coming on strong. She felt dizzy with sudden concern. Nothing had truly changed between herself and Ian, just the strange blood rose phenomenon that had clipped her at the back of her knees.

She saw movement from the corner of her eye and shifted to see if an owl had flown out over the gorge. But what was actually there sent fear pummeling her heart. A red wind flowed down near the cliffs, the truest sign deadly wraith-pairs were headed their way.

She returned to Ian and waved her hand at him, drawing his attention back to her.

"Invictus," she said, gesturing to the southern vista.

Ian followed the line of her arm. "I see the wind." To Ben, he said, "I'm switching to telepathy. We're in trouble here."

He shoved his phone back into his pocket and she sensed he was now pathing to Ben.

Looking up at his face, she could see he stared out at the gorge, then slowly turned to view the farthest western horizon, the southern cliff, then the eastern flow of land in the direction of the Leberion Plain.

Finally, he turned to her. *Regan, I won't pretend we're not in trouble. By my best guess, having fought the Invictus for centuries, we're looking at twenty pair and they're headed straight for us. Ben's sending the Guard. Ten will be here in a few minutes, with an additional thirty arriving after that.*

What do we do until then? she pathed.

Hold them off.

Even during the time they'd been together, she'd never been in a real battle situation with Ian. She felt his tension as though every muscle in his body was flexed, ready and waiting.

He lifted his arm, staring down at the blood tattoos. "Do you know what this means?"

She looked at his arms. Each line now pulsed. She lifted her own arms and it was the same thing, as though the marks were alive. "We've both agreed this is power, but I don't know what it is or what I'm supposed to do with it."

"Same here, but we'll figure it out. Right now we have to hunker down." He caught her arm and guided her back into the house, closing the sliding glass door and locking it.

He began moving furniture, pushing the sofas and chairs up against the curved windows. "The glass is bullet-proof, but with this many pairs, I don't know what we'll be up against."

"Can I help? What about the steel shutters?"

"That's next, because it will slow the enemy down. But most of the shutters are set at a distance from the house. Any of the Invictus can slip between."

As he moved toward the foyer, he gestured with a quick wave of his hand for her to join him. She didn't have to be told twice, but ran to his side.

He took her hand. "Stick close."

"I will."

Moving across the foyer, then turning into the hall leading to the bedrooms and the library, he opened the control box. He flipped the switch to override the automatic commands and pressed the shutter button. The sudden sound of the shutters lowering made her jump again as they had the first time.

The next moment, there was an awful banging on the steel, gaining in volume as more and more hands struck the metal. What followed was worse as several wraiths started to shriek in the horrible way the Invictus wraiths could.

"Oh, God." She covered her ears.

But he took her hands away, forcing her to hear the thunder-like sounds. "You need to be strong, Regan. We're in it right now and this noise is nothing; it's only meant to frighten you, but don't let it." He kept hold of her right hand. "Okay. Back to the living room."

"Why there?"

"Because if any of these Invictus have enough battle energy to bust down the windows, we'll have room to fight."

"We?" She swallowed hard.

He lifted her arm. "Do you see how your marks are pulsing? They're matching mine and what I've accessed is my battle energy, the vibration I can release when I engage the Invictus. And I believe you're also experiencing a ramped up version of battle power."

Regan stared at her arms, then closed her eyes, shutting out the terrible din of fists striking steel. She wanted to know exactly what he meant and to feel the energy herself.

A new vibration had started to pulse and it had Ian's signature. She was feeling his battle power as well as her own since every realm-person had essential battle ability. She'd just never accessed hers before.

Opening her eyes, she turned and gripped Ian's hand. "You're right. But what should I do? This is all new to me."

He held her gaze tightly. "Go with your instincts every step of the way. When the time comes, you'll know what action to take. Be strong."

She deliberately straightened her shoulders and forced herself to grow calm.

In response, he offered a crooked smile, then kissed her once on the lips. "You'll do."

She hoped to hell he was right.

The pounding on the shutters and the shrieks of the wraiths got louder and louder then suddenly stopped.

"Did someone issue an order or something?" she asked.

"I'm sure of it."

"I've always thought of the Invictus pairs as completely unruly."

"Not anymore. Margetta has found a way to harness them, to control them."

Suddenly, several Invictus pairs slid between the steel shutters and the bank of curved glass windows. The wraiths' eyes glowed a fierce red hue and their bonded mates, whether troll or fae, vampire or shifter, appeared crazed. Each began to hammer on the glass for effect, to make noise to frighten them. A couple of massive shifters threw their weight against the windows. Their combined battle energies could have busted the bullet-proof glass, but noise was something wraith-pairs loved to make.

Ian held up his right hand and let his battle energy flow. He erected a massive blue shield in front of the two of them, his power crackling the air.

Regan wished like anything she had Olivia's ability to create a shield of invisibility. But for all her power as the Ruby Fae and the realm knowledge she shared on a daily basis with her fae students, she couldn't do much in a battle situation.

Just when she was sure it couldn't get worse, she felt Ian tense up. "Shit," he muttered.

"What? What now?" Glancing up at him, she followed the direction of his gaze.

Ian was staring at a large vampire and his bonded wraith. The woman levitated, her dark black hair writhing as though a strong wind swirled around her. She wore the red gauzy strips of fabric pieced together in a long gown-like garment, a design common among the female wraiths. The woman smiled, bearing sharp yellow fangs.

Her vampire mate wore only leathers and tough-looking black boots with steel toes. His heavily muscled chest was bare.

As she watched him, understanding came to her and she inched closer to Ian. The vampire was a mastyr. Because he was bonded with a wraith, he would have gained an extraordinary amount of power, well beyond Ian's level.

If they'd been in trouble before, they were now close to the pit of hell. There was no question in her mind that this mastyr could defeat Ian.

"Holy fuck," Ian murmured.

At first, she thought he was expressing his own dismay. Instead, she sensed it was something else. "Wait. You know him, don't you?"

"Braden. He was one of mine and I thought him long dead. Looks like he's been serving Margetta instead. I knew he'd coveted my position, and there'd even been rumors he'd bought some black market fae spells to ramp up his power. But he never succeeded in besting me or Ben for that matter. Now here he is."

Regan watched in horror as Braden lifted both fists, his Invictus red battle energy glowing like fire over both hands. He waved an arm and shouted an order. The frenzied Invictus pairs all slid away from between the windows and the steel shutters so that Braden and his hovering wraith stood alone behind the glass.

Braden summoned the full breadth of his power. He was a big vampire and all muscle, almost matching Ian's size. His long, wavy black hair hung loose past his shoulders. With his lips pulled back over sharp fangs and his skin now a dark maroon color, he looked beyond ferocious, ready to kill.

Regan was surprised she wasn't shaking like mad, except she felt something emanating from Ian, a kind of calm that could only come from a man who'd made war for centuries. In this difficult moment, she felt all that he was, the force of his will, his determination, and his stature as a Vampire Guardsman.

Despite Braden's amplified power, because of the wraith bond, Ian knew what he was doing.

Ian pathed. *This is damn good news, Regan. Braden wants to take me on alone. He could have commanded the field right now if he'd kept even two of the Invictus pairs close by. Instead, he's throwing down the gauntlet.*

Regan felt tears burn her eyes. Basically, Ian had just told her they now had a chance.

Thank the Goddess.

Amen to that.

He released her hand and moved to stand three feet in front of her, yet still twenty feet away from the windows. His blue battle shield shimmered the full length of the living room.

Stay well back.

She drew a deep breath. *That's the plan.*

Braden, his battle vibrations at full-bore, planted his fists against the window, and let the same energy invade the thick glass. She watched large fissures form, then with another wave of power, a thousand smaller cracks.

One more burst of his energy and all the panels of the glass wall shattered.

When Braden levitated slowly, flying above the furniture to land not far from Ian's blue shield, she knew then Ian had been right; Braden wanted to go *mano-a-mano* with Ian.

But could Ian hold his own long enough for Ben's troops to get here in time?

~ ~ ~

"Come on, motherfucker. Bring it." Ian's vision had narrowed to the traitor who'd once served in his Vampire Guard, but who had since sold his soul to the devil.

Braden lifted both hands and engaged his own battle energy. Red sparks flew at Ian's shield.

Ian pressed back, holding his blue energy tight, but Braden's power pulsed heavy and strong. Ian knew he couldn't hold out against the vampire's enhanced ability for very long. So, rather than waste his resources on holding the shield, he chose to let it go and slowly allowed the blue vibrating wall to disintegrate.

But Ian had more than one reason for giving ground. He would be able keep Regan safer this way since he could then control the physical battle with Braden better. And he could buy time for his troops to arrive.

Braden offered a slow triumphant smile in return. He moved forward, his maniacal, Invictus gaze fixed on Ian. "I've been waiting for this day a long time. So make it good, Ian. I want you bruised all to hell when I finally smash the last bit of life out of your face."

Ian, his arm muscles flexing, lifted both hands in a pair of fists, grateful as never before that he wore his rings. He'd need every single one of them this night.

He began with a taunt. "Had to suck up to a wraith to get the balls you need to fight? Is that it, traitor?"

Braden's lips curled, and he launched at Ian. He moved fast and caught Ian in the stomach. Ian flew back, landing with a heavy thud against a support beam, but remained standing.

Braden drew back enough to wind up for a serious right hook. But Ian had been around a few decades and before Braden's fist could land, he smashed Braden's ribs with two quick hits. As

Braden doubled over, Ian levitated backward just far enough that when he swung his booted foot, he landed a powerful kick in Braden's gut.

Braden grunted, then in a swift flash of movement, tucked, rolled and gained his feet a couple yards away from Ian. Braden didn't rush in again, as he had because of Ian's taunt. Instead, though breathing hard and protecting his left side with his elbow, he danced on his feet, side-stepping several times.

Ian knew Braden was doing a quick self-heal. He watched the large bruising on the vampire's bare stomach diminish steadily then vanish. So much power.

Ian held back, moving his shoulders slowly, fists up. His gaze never left Braden. Stalling was good.

Braden moved in again, only faster than before. He swept past Ian on his right and in the same split-second turned and caught Ian in a choke-hold.

Ian reacted instinctively by grabbing the heavy muscular arm pressing against his windpipe. But he'd never be able to break the hold with his hands.

He mentally regrouped quickly, shifted sideways just enough to slam his elbow into Braden's ribs. The jolt caused Braden to reduce the pressure on Ian's neck.

Ian caught Braden's arm in a tough grasp, then with a jerk of his hips and legs, flipped Braden over his head.

Braden landed hard on his back. Ian felt the vibrations up both legs since the entire building shook. Braden had to be close to three hundred pounds.

Again, Ian drew back several feet, needing more than anything to buy some time. But the next second, Braden rushed him while levitating, spun and kicked Ian hard in the face. Ian flew backward, his head hitting the stone hearth in front of the fireplace.

"Ian," Regan cried out.

Ian slowly rose onto his knees, shaking his head. The kick had hurt like hell and his brain felt like it was upside down. He couldn't pull his thoughts together. He needed time. But he didn't get it, since Braden offered up his own heavy boot and kicked Ian repeatedly in the abdomen.

Ian drew himself into a knot, taking the blows, but he couldn't do much more than that. His head throbbed badly.

When Braden shifted, and began kicking him in the spine, the blows added a whole new level of pain to the mix.

~ ~ ~

Regan had watched the battle with her heart in her throat. Because Braden kept pounding Ian with his boot, she knew she had to do something or Ian would die.

Her forearms vibrated powerfully with Ian's battle energy. He'd said to go with her instincts so without giving it too much thought, Regan levitated and flew at lightning speed toward Braden. Just before she made contact, she flipped, kicked out with both feet while in a horizontal line and connected hard with the back of Braden's skull. He flew against the fireplace, his forehead hitting the mantel. Down he went.

The force of her kick sent her flying backward. But she accessed her levitation skill quickly and broke her fall, landing not far from Ian.

Sitting up quickly, she placed a hand on his forearm over what she now thought of as blood tattoos. She gathered her healing vibration and let it flow. She was stunned by the level of power she was able to release and could feel it moving into Ian in a swift wave. A few seconds later, Ian sat up, his gray eyes wide as he stared at her.

Holy shit, Regan. Your power. You're healing me.

She nodded, but her attention was caught by Braden next to her, now righting himself and levitating. She had to get out of the way and started to rise up when hands caught her from behind.

Suddenly airborne, she realized the bonded wraith had engaged the battle as well. She launched Regan with tremendous Invictus power toward the windows.

Regan would have hit one of the steel frames, but she was able at the last moment to reverse her course, charting a safer trajectory back into the room. Even so, she hit the floor hard.

Shaken, she still forced herself to levitate, to gain her bearings. Ian was back to battling Braden, but where was the wraith?

She caught sight of a red flash above her. The next instant, the wraith screeched and fell on Regan, pushing her on her back as she took her down to the wood floor.

Power flowed from the wraith, a vibration she knew was all vampire because the woman had blended her being with Braden. She sat on Regan, pinning her down and using each of her hands to keep Regan's arms from moving. Regan was completely helpless against the woman's superior physical strength.

She lifted Regan's arms and crossed them at the wrists. Using only one of her hands, the wraith grabbed both wrists, holding Regan captive. In a clever maneuver, the wraith used Regan's hands, pressing them to Regan's face in order to force her head to the side.

No. Oh, no. Sweet Goddess, no!

From her peripheral vision, Regan saw the woman's sharp fangs emerge. Invictus wraiths, given their maniacal state, were brutal feeders. The next moment, the wraith struck Regan's throat with a swift, hard, painful blow. Opening the vein, she began to drink in deep gulps that had Regan crying out in agony.

Wraiths took blood the same way vampires did, except that an Invictus wraith drank until there was so little left the heart stopped beating.

Worse. Each sip powered the wraith even more.

Fear became a cloud in Regan's head, paralyzing her mind and preventing her from doing anything.

Regan could hear Ian and Braden battling, so she knew she couldn't rely on help from that quarter. She had to do something, or she would die this very night and she didn't want to, especially not by the fangs of a heinous bonded wraith.

She forced her breathing to ease and despite the pain and fear, she entered a meditative state. Slowly, her mind began to function again and her thoughts started coming together. Each fae had a different set of abilities. Vojalie had said she didn't excel at spell-making, but Regan did.

She also had something else: Ian's blood tattoos on her arms offering her power to tap into.

She focused on these things and a moment later new thoughts emerged. For one thing, her blood. The wraith was drinking her blood.

Regan kept the power of the tattoos flowing and combined those strong vibrations with a focus on the bile in her body. She conjured a simple spell and though she might be ill afterwards, she could feel bile filling her stomach. With the power she now had through the blood tattoos, she let the bile leak into her blood stream a little at first, then a lot.

A few seconds later, the wraith leaped off her, spewing a mouthful of Regan's blood. A shriek followed, then she fell to the ground, rolling back and forth.

Regan was unsteady as she levitated. Once more, Braden had the upper hand and pummeled Ian. She had to intervene. If she could kill the wraith, the vampire would lose his bonded power and Ian would be able to defeat Braden.

Searching through the jumbled living room, she found a heavy pewter candlestick, flew toward it, and as soon as she had it in hand, turned and headed back to the wraith. Though gasping for air, the woman gained her feet.

Regan pathed to Ian. *I'm taking the bitch down. Be ready.*

Though she was sick to her stomach and her veins were on fire because of the bile, she jerked the candlestick up in a swift arc, and caught the wraith beneath her chin. The wraith flew backward, eyes fluttering. Her head connected with one of the steel window frames and she sank to the floor, unconscious.

Regan moved swiftly to where the wraith lay. Her spine was twisted and she was barely breathing, but she was still alive.

Regan had never been presented with this kind of problem before. She held the candlestick in her hand and had to make a decision, maybe the hardest she'd ever made.

She'd never killed anyone in the course of her life, but did she dare let the wraith live?

Her heart slammed around in her chest. Wraiths by nature weren't evil, only when they'd been turned by Margetta's foul means into an Invictus being.

Holding the candlestick in an iron grip, she turned to see how Ian fared. An Invictus pair gained strength from each other in a constant flow of energy. Because the wraith was unconscious, Regan could tell that Braden had lost a good portion of his power. Ian now sat on the man's chest and threw punch after punch, his rings helping to deliver a well-deserved beating. The mastyr was also nearly unconscious as well.

She also heard sounds of a battle heating up outside the house. Relief flooded her since she knew the troops Ben had sent had finally arrived and were now engaging the rest of Braden's Invictus force.

Ian, she pathed, turning in his direction. *I can't do this. I'm sorry, but I can't kill her.*

Ian rose up. Braden lay on his back, his face bloody, and he wasn't moving.

Ian was breathing hard as he looked at her over his shoulder. *I wondered why Braden had suddenly succumbed. And you did this?* He waved a hand in the direction of the prone wraith.

Yes, through the power of the blood tattoo, but I can't finish her off.

I understand. What I want you to do is to put your hand on top of her head and release a small flow of battle energy. I'll do the same here. That will keep each of them unconscious until we can get a retrieval squad from Bergisson over here.

Really? Tears burned Regan's eyes; she wouldn't have to kill the woman after all.

Yes.

Are you sure?

I am. Absolutely. I know how much this would hurt you and what you've just been through is bad enough.

In all her long-lived life, Regan had never made use of her battle vibration until tonight. Earlier, she'd made use of Ian's, but never her own. With it, she could stream energy powerful enough to hurt and even kill others.

She placed her hand on top of the wraith's head and let the smallest amount possible leave her hand. When it entered the wraith, the woman seized, moaning faintly, then her whole body went lax.

Regan sensed the wraith would be out for hours.

Shifting to glance at Ian who stood over Braden, she could see that Ian had put the traitorous vampire in the same state as his bonded mate, as though resting in a deep trance.

It was over.

She had blood all over her clothes from the wraith spewing Regan's tainted blood. Ian was bleeding from several cuts and was bruised in a dozen different places.

But they were both alive.

"Regan, I'm sorry you had to go through this."

She crossed to him and when she drew close, he opened his arms. She all but threw herself against his chest and held him tight around the waist. She didn't care they were both a mess. She let the tears flow.

She was also nauseous from the bile and needed to cleanse her blood or she'd really be ill. For now, though, she needed Ian's comforting embrace more than anything.

Ben's voice flowed into the space. "We've got the Invictus out here contained and Ethan's team is on its way. A number are dead, but I'd say we have ten pairs we'll be sending on to Bergisson Realm. Eleven, including these two." With her face buried against

Ian's chest, she couldn't see Ben, but she knew him well. He was Ian's number-two Guardsman and almost as powerful as Ian. Camberlaune was fortunate to have two such powerful mastyrs serving the realm.

"That's good." Ian's chest rumbled as he spoke, his deep voice easing her a little more.

Later, when the retrieval team arrived to take Braden and his bonded mate away, Regan went into the kitchen and drank two large glasses of water. She then invoked another spell and set about removing the bile from her blood. She also encouraged Ian to be with his Guardsmen especially since she needed some time alone.

She went into the bathroom of her guest room, intending to wipe down. But when she saw how much blood spatter she had on her face, neck and in her hair, she stripped down and stepped into the shower. She let the warm water flow, then focused inward on her blood to continue the cleansing process.

By the time she toweled off, put on fresh clothes, and set about drying her hair, she felt more like herself, just really sober, even grief-stricken from having gotten this close to the war.

Chapter Five

A half hour later, Ian hovered in the air near the gorge cliff. The retrieval team had come and gone and now his men were doing a search for those Invictus who'd been struck down midair and fallen into the gorge.

Three trolls, already planted in the afterlife, had been brought up and now lay in a row at the edge of the cliff. Their bonded wraiths lay near them as well, also dead.

There would be more to come.

It was tough seeing them stretched out. Each Realm-person had most likely been abducted and the bond forced on them. When it happened, these men and women became beast-like versions of themselves and anxious to make war.

The Invictus fought with a ferocity matched only by trained Guardsmen or those shifters belonging to any of the Nine Realm Brigades.

Aware how much he owed his second-in-command, Ian stood next to Ben. "Thanks for getting the troops here as fast as you did. You saved my ass."

"Grateful as hell we got here in time." He glanced at the house. "But you'll need new digs."

"I've thought of that. I'm going to take Regan to my cabin." He should have taken her there in the first place. It was in the far northeastern part of his realm and high in the mountains. Given the distance from Margetta's fortress on the border between Camberlaune and Stone's realm, he was pretty sure he'd be free from any kind of Invictus attacks.

No one knew where his cabin was except for one fae caretaker who lived several miles to the south of the dwelling and could be trusted to keep the place a secret.

He hadn't even shared the location with Ben, or the name of his caretaker, and he intended to keep it that way. He often went to his mountain retreat after a grueling night when too many of his people died and not enough Invictus had been saved to send to Bergisson for rehab.

Right now, after almost dying at the hands of a wraith-bonded mastyr, he wanted Regan in his arms and the wind in his face as he flew northeast for about seventy miles.

Stone appeared suddenly, topping the edge of the cliff, a dead female troll in his arms. Ian understood the hard expression on his face, especially since the troll wore slave chains pierced through her ears and nose. A lot of his Realm-folk were abducted and forced into slavery first. Later, they'd have to endure bonding with a wraith and the subsequent vaporizing of personality, long held beliefs, and basic Realm decency. As a result, most of those wraith-bonded would eventually die during a battle with his Vampire Guard or his Brigade.

Ian needed the war over.

Stone laid the body next to a wraith. He rose, but remained where he was, his eyes closed. He was probably offering up a prayer of supplication to the Goddess to take her servant despite the sins of the wraith-bond. Ian had done the same thousands of times over the centuries.

He crossed his arms over his chest and stared out across the gorge to the opposite cliff, beyond the tree line and into the southern night sky. A bright glow of stars burned along what he knew to be the Milky Way.

His world shared the earth's universe on a separate yet joined plane. His access point was Harrisburg, a city in Pennsylvania. He had a communication center there. Ben had seen to the construction and later the overall operations.

Yet very few humans visited his realm anymore, not with so many Invictus attacks in Camberlaune.

Stone moved to stand on Ian's right. "Looks like they were after you or maybe Regan."

"I'm thinking both of us. I knew the mastyr; he'd served in my Guard for a long time. When he disappeared several years ago, I thought he was dead. Instead, he'd joined Margetta's army."

"Fuck." He then glanced at Ian, frowning. "How the hell did you defeat him? His power must have been off the charts because he was wraith-bonded."

"It was and actually I almost bought it, but Regan intervened. I'm not sure how she did it, especially since the bonded wraith attacked her." He held up his arms. "We've been sharing power, though, because of these."

Stone peered at his arms. "What the hell is this?"

Ian explained.

Stone shook his head slowly. "And this allowed Regan to defeat a wraith. Sweet Goddess."

Ian turned to glance at the house, at the shattered windows. Regan was inside somewhere. "To my knowledge, this is the closest she's ever been to a battle."

Stone sighed heavily. "I don't think I'll ever understand this whole blood rose thing that puts our women in harm's way. It's not fair to them."

"No, it's not."

"What's the plan, Ian? You're not staying here."

"No. I'm taking Regan to my cabin for the rest of the night. She'll be safe there." He rubbed his forehead, thinking hard. "But we've got to find some way of locating Margetta's fortress. It's damn time we went on the offensive."

"I've been thinking the same thing. Not sure how to get the job done, though, when there's a powerful shielding mist problem like the one you described." Stone met his gaze. "What about Regan? This should be up her alley. And I know the things the mastyrs have said, those bonded to blood roses. There always seems to be a task the pair must accomplish together. Maybe this is yours."

"I don't know," Ian said. He didn't want it to be true. He'd protect Regan for the time being, but as soon as it was safe, he wanted her back in Swanicott and for his own life to get back to normal.

Stone pressed him. "Think about it. Every blood rose couple has become a team. Look at Ethan and Samantha. Together, they rehabilitate Invictus pairs. We've been able to save realm-folk now because of Samantha's blood rose gift." He gestured to the south, in the general direction of Swanicott Realm. "And Olivia can shield Zane besides creating a Zephyr wind in battle. Maybe you and Regan will be able to establish the coordinates for Margetta's army, I mean if you worked together."

Ian ground his molars. "You know how I feel about her. Our history is bad."

"I know, and I sympathize. But I have to speak my mind, Ian, because if you could find Margetta's army, then maybe you and I together could take her on. It would be a start."

Was it possible? If he worked with Regan, could the two of them together start bringing the war to an end?

Stone turned his head in a westerly direction. His realm lay two hundred miles from Ian's home, directly west. He shook his head slowly. "I've flown over that region thousands of times, over the border between our realms. But I've never seen a damn thing, not even the mist you've talked about."

"I'd never seen it either, not until Margetta abducted Regan."

His gaze flipped back to Ian. "Another sign."

Ian didn't want to admit it, but Stone had a point. Why hadn't Ian been able to see Margetta's mist until now?

Stone muttered a curse. "All this time, so close to my realm."

"I know the feeling."

With his mind made up to take Regan to his cabin, Ian turned to Ben and talked over how the rest of the night would be handled. Ben told him not to worry, he'd keep a fourth of the Guard on patrol where the gorge ended and the plain began. He also expressed the opinion he thought it likely the attack at Ian's home had been prompted by Braden alone and wasn't an opening salvo to a full-scale war against Camberlaune.

Ian had to agree. If Margetta had been intent on conquering his realm, she wouldn't have sent a couple dozen Invictus pairs to his home; she would have sent her army full bore down into the Leberion plain.

So why hadn't she done just that? Too many damn questions, not enough answers. He also kept mulling over Regan's observation that Margetta wasn't behaving like she was up against the ropes.

All the speculation, however, wouldn't change what he needed to do next.

He turned to Stone and clapped him on the shoulder. "If you have ideas about how we should move forward, I want to hear them."

"I've been thinking of nothing else."

"Is it time to contact the queen? Hell, from what I've heard, Rosamunde has her land shrouded in a similar kind of shielding mist."

Stone frowned. "Actually, I spoke with her earlier."

"You called her?"

"She called me. She's had a premonition Margetta is building to something big."

It wasn't so long ago that Mastyr Quinlan had discovered the queen living in a shielded land between the borders of Grochaire Realm and Walvashorr. She was over a thousand years old and had essentially been in hiding for most of that time. A few rumors were rife she was related to Margetta, but nothing had been proven. Ian had once asked Davido if he knew of a kinship between Rosamunde and Margetta, but the ancient troll had avoided answering the question.

"Will Rosamunde get involved?" Ian asked. "If she can create a similar shielding mist to Margetta's, maybe she could bust through this one near the gorge. Will you at least ask?"

At that, Stone's nostrils flared. The brother was angry.

"What?"

"I already did. The queen refused."

"I don't understand," Ian said. "Why?"

"Basically, she's convinced this isn't her battle, otherwise she would have jumped in sooner, as in centuries ago. She said it's a fae thing and she's not to be involved."

Ian knew better than to question Rosamunde's decision. The fae of the Nine Realms had to answer to their highest calling first and sometimes that meant counter-intuitive decision-making.

"Ian?" Regan's voice had him turning in her direction, Stone as well. She stood on the porch, her striped satchel in hand, but she wore a different set of clothes. The battle-stained lot had been covered in blood. She now wore a long, violet sweater and jeans, though she'd put on her ankle boots again.

Her thick, light brown hair was parted in the middle and hung in a mass around her shoulders. It appeared to be damp. No doubt she'd needed to shower after the battle with the wraith.

His heart felt strangely compressed as he looked at her and desire rose once more.

"Ready when you are," she said.

"Give me a sec?"

"Absolutely." She set the satchel down on the front step and nodded.

His forearms felt heated, and looking down, he saw the tattoos were glowing. Regan's appearance had activated the tattoos. The problem was, they also made him acutely aware that Stone was a mastyr vampire and would crave Regan the way Ian did. Ben, as well.

He backed away from both Guardsmen, glancing from one to the other.

"Holy shit," Stone muttered. "They're alive, aren't they?"

"Part of my skin now." Against his rational mind, Ian's battle vibration fired up and his fangs thrummed in his gums. Despite the protection the tattoos offered, on a primal level he was preparing to defend Regan against other potential contenders.

Because Stone was the more powerful of the two mastyrs, he held Stone's gaze, his shoulders hunched, but Stone only smiled. "I think the blood tattoos are working for you, because I'm not feeling a thing toward Regan."

"Me, neither," Ben added.

Still, Ian's words came out on a growl as he shifted his gaze once more between the men. "Let's keep it that way."

Stone took a step back and tossed up both hands in a gesture of surrender as did Ben.

Ian forced himself to calm down. He couldn't believe how fast he'd been ready to do battle with Stone again. Ben as well, if needed.

He took several deep breaths and forced his battle energy to dial down. When he felt under control once more, he turned to Ben. "Call me on my cell if you need me, especially if Margetta makes a move against Camberlaune. I can be back in a few minutes."

Ben nodded. "I've got this, Ian. Just take care of the Ruby Fae."

Ian took one last look around at his Vampire Guard doing a final clean-up. They only waited now for the troll dispatch crew to arrive and ship the dead to the local morgue.

He knew he didn't need to stay a moment longer, yet he hated leaving a battle scene. Camberlaune was his responsibility.

Stone spoke in a low voice. "Be with her, Ian. Ben and I have this covered. I'm sticking around until we know the Ancient Fae's next move. I've already put all the ruling mastyrs on alert as well. If we need to mobilize, we're ready."

Ian could finally breathe. With both Stone and Ben in charge, his concern for his realm eased, and he could now turn his attention to Regan.

Heading toward the porch, he felt the blood tattoos still sending pulses of heat up his arms. As he drew close, Regan's rich scent reminded him of her earlier words that she was all in. He sure as hell hoped so because given the way her jasmine-lime scent had him worked up, he would have the devil of a time keeping his hands off her. Especially since for the next few hours, he'd have her all to himself in an isolated location.

"Everything set?" she asked, searching his eyes.

He told her about his cabin, and he couldn't mistake the glint in her dark brown eyes. As he caught her arm, a different kind of vibration, very sexual in nature, moved over her skin.

"Regan," he said quietly. "I don't want to take advantage of you."

"It's okay," she whispered. "I'm willing and that's all you need to know."

Another potent rush of desire traveled from his groin, straight up through his body until blood pounded in his head. He almost took her in his arms, but he was battle-stained, his woman had just showered, and they had an audience.

He took her hand and led her back into his house, taking her with him to his master bedroom. "I want to kiss you, but not like this. I won't be long."

"Again, ready when you are."

The words had a double meaning, and he almost hauled her into his arms anyway. Instead, he made tracks for the bathroom, stripped down like his feet were on fire, removed all ten rings, then hopped in the shower.

~ ~ ~

Regan felt tingly all over, from the soft vibrations traveling down her neck and sides, to the exquisite sensations playing over her sex.

She had to work hard to recall the last time she'd been with a man. After a moment, she realized it had been eight years. She'd dated a fae professor for a few months. He'd been a good man and had satisfied her in bed. But when images of Ian kept creeping into her mind during sex, she decided to break it off. She didn't have enough passion to continue the relationship, but *eight years* was a long time.

Tonight would end a severe dry spell.

When she realized she'd remained in one place with her satchel still clutched in her fingers, she dropped the bag and sat down on the bench at the end of Ian's bed.

She was glad he'd brought her with him into the bedroom. The sight of Stone had unsettled her, even though it was clear the blood tattoos had done their work and the powerful mastyr had barely given her a cursory glance.

Ian's bedroom had a similar view to the library since it overlooked the western vista. The steel shutters had long since been raised following the battle and her night vision warmed up the landscape. The granite outcropping on which the house sat provided an unobstructed view of the angled portion of the gorge.

As the shower droned, she left the bed to have a good look.

The cliff opposite had striations of rock, one after another with variations of beige, gray, a thin line of black and even red. She'd always loved Dark Gorge for its natural beauty and the feeling of power inherent in the rugged cliffs. The river below, that serviced most of the plain cities of the realm, had cut through the rock over the millennia.

A quarter mile away was a beautiful wrought-iron bridge. She watched as shifters in their wolf form moved from the southern cliff to the northern, then disappeared along several trails leading into the mountains. She loved her world, the beauty of the land and the unique aspect of each species, which only made Margetta's corruption of the usually gentle wraith spirit one of the most heinous in the Nine Realms' long history.

When the shower shut off, she turned in the direction of the bathroom, where steam flowed into the dressing area.

Ian emerged, a towel around his waist, his dark hair hanging wet to the middle of his back.

Her lips parted. His warrior physique was so beautiful and so perfect. His shoulders were broad and heavily muscled, and his back angled to a narrow, fit waist. The towel covered a tight gorgeous ass and her hands involuntarily made a pair of claws because she knew when and how she wanted to sink her nails, something he'd always enjoyed.

"See something you like?"

She lifted her gaze from his backside and saw that he'd caught her watching him from the mirror above the sink.

Busted.

But she wasn't embarrassed. Instead, she crossed the room coming up behind him and slid her hands around his waist. She wasn't a short woman, but Ian was six-six, so she had to peer around his shoulder to meet his gaze in the mirror. *I was just thinking about how I used to use my nails. Remember?*

His whole body did a strange rolling jerk. *Sweet Goddess, yes.*

She released him and he leaned forward, catching his hands on the edge of the sink. He'd been in the middle of putting his rings on and now took deep breaths. *I want to kiss you and do everything else right now. But if I get started, I won't be able to stop.*

She laughed and headed back to the bedroom window. *I'd better be good, then, because I really don't want to stay in this house as beautiful as it is.*

When Ian lost the towel, however, desire shot through her sex once more and created a kind of whirling effect between her legs. She almost ran to him and leaped on his back.

But he was right. Once either of them got going nothing would stop them. Worse, there'd probably be a dozen Guardsmen outside who'd hear a whole lot of moans, sighs, and at least one earth-shattering scream she knew would come from her throat.

So she turned away from him and even closed her eyes as she worked to focus on anything else. "Just let me know when you're dressed. Okay?"

He chuckled, a deep throaty sound. "Almost done." A moment later, "There. You're safe now."

But as she shifted to face him, she knew she was anything but safe. He wore jeans and a long-sleeved t-shirt and looked more handsome than ever. Her heart was in danger of falling for Ian all over again. Everything he was as a warrior, as a devoted leader of his realm, as a trusted friend to those closest to him was what she admired most in a man. In some ways, Ian was her ideal.

In others, as in how much he blamed her for the massacre at Raven's Overlook, she knew she had little hope this could ever be more than a brief interlude.

Sex with Ian would be amazing; it always had been.

But beyond a beautiful laying together, what future could she possibly have with him?

He came to her and took her hands. "I know you're distressed; I can feel it in the air. Was it the battle?"

She shook her head. She could have said so many things right now, but held back. She could even have spoken the words, 'Raven's Overlook', and ended this moment with Ian entirely. In doing so, she wouldn't have to worry about the future of her already achy heart.

Instead, she made a decision then and there not to let her concern for *what might happen* destroy the next few hours with Ian.

Taking a deep breath, she told a half-lie. "I'm worried about what Margetta is planning to do next."

He pulled her against him, wrapping his strong arms around her shoulders and back. She moaned softly. "You don't know how good that feels."

~ ~ ~

She was wrong; he did know. Regan felt like heaven in his arms because she fit him really well and he never felt as though she'd break if he squeezed too hard. She had a full figure with rounded curves and large breasts.

And he needed her in his bed.

Without saying another word, he released her to pick up her satchel. Afterward, he took her hand. She walked beside him to the front door with a hop to her step. She seemed to be as anxious as he was to get going. But for what he wanted to do to her, he needed some privacy. No way in hell he wanted even one of the Guardsmen privy to his doings with Regan.

Once outside, he settled her on his right boot with his arm around her waist and held her tight against him. He inclined his head first to Ben, then Stone. After which, he levitated straight up, then headed east until he was well out of sight of any of the Guard.

When he felt certain no one could see him, he veered north angling his flight at the foothills of the Dauphaire Mountains, staying to the contours of the land. He passed over several villages, but maintained his altitude so that he and Regan wouldn't be seen.

Regan was quiet, though she sighed several times, leaning her head against his neck. She'd always loved flying with him. How many times had she asked him to take her for a quick flight for the sheer pleasure of it? She trusted him — that much he knew — and he valued her confidence in him.

Sweet Goddess, he needed to take her to bed. His drive toward her was almost overwhelming and everything he'd read on the loop or heard the other mastyrs say about the blood rose experience now made complete sense to him. Mostly, he was struck by the powerful need he felt to protect her, as though her essential value to him had increased exponentially.

But how could he and this woman ever truly have a life together? She'd enthralled him, or at least he'd always believed she had. And because of that thrall, over two hundred villagers at Raven's Overlook had died.

Yes, he blamed her. He'd tried to leave her bed repeatedly that night, knowing he needed to be with his Vampire Guard, but she'd kept calling him back.

And he'd gone to her because he couldn't help himself. If that wasn't enthrallment, then what was it?

He'd lived with centuries of guilt for having been so weak and here he was again, caught in a similar drive to be with Regan. Only this time, a phenomenon had hold of him, something other mastyrs had experienced.

He also knew he had to be open to the power their connection could bring. From the same conversations and loop emails with the bonded mastyrs, he knew unexpected powers could emerge, abilities with great potential for use against the Ancient Fae.

When he reached the foothill village of Juniango, he veered west and began the climb in altitude to 5000 feet. Regan's warm body pressed up against his, kept his need for her thrumming strong, despite the serious questions he had about their relationship.

The battle with Braden had drained him. He needed to make love to Regan and to feed again. Whether he liked it or not, she was a blood rose and he'd made a commitment to take the journey with her as far as he could.

He knew she had her doubts as well, which kept his conscience clear.

When he topped the final rise, he flew down into a large green meadow. The cabin was perched between a meadow and a small river. Behind the cabin was the typical Dauphaire mixed forest.

A hot spring bubbled from the top of the meadow at the western end, flowing in a shallow stream to the river. He often used the spring to ease sore muscles after a hard night of battling, then bathed in the river at the point the spring emptied its superheated contents into the cold water of the river.

He slowed his flight as he headed to the front porch.

"Ian, you have a paradise here."

He smiled. "I do. And in case you're concerned, only my caretaker, whom I trust with my life, knows about this property.

He's stocked the fridge for us and I think he said he's provided a dish of his wife's homemade lasagna."

"Sounds like heaven."

As he dropped to the wide, wood walkway that overlooked the river, she stepped off his foot and turned to view the broad rush of water. "I'd be here all the time. I mean, I enjoy the location of my fae retreat, but we don't have anything like this nearby." She leaned on the handrail, peering over the side.

He drew up next to her. His gaze lifted to the rising moon, and he was reminded again what Regan's blood had done for him. "I'm still amazed I don't need the sunglasses anymore. This amount of light would have given me a serious headache." He twisted his thumb ring. "I'm grateful, Regan. I want you to know that."

She glanced at him as he settled his forearms on the thick wood, then rubbed his shoulder. "I'm grateful as well. It was always hard for me knowing how you suffered, but I could never do a thing about it."

He nodded, holding her gaze. "You have a good heart."

Her lips curved in a soft smile then she shifted her attention back to the river.

He did the same, taking a moment to enjoy the sound of the river, the small white-caps as the current hit immoveable stones, the glimmer of moonlight reflected in the water.

As often happened when he came here, he found he could breathe. Of course it helped that Stone was in Camberlaune and would take care of anything the Invictus might throw at his realm through the rest of the night.

After several minutes of shared appreciation, he turned to her. "Hungry?" he asked.

She nodded, smiling. "Starved, especially since you mentioned lasagna."

A few minutes later, he had two plates loaded with the warmed up, layered Italian casserole, a pair of forks, and two glasses of wine settled on the table by the deck window.

Regan had never stopped looking outside. She held a glass of wine to her lips and even now her gaze slid to the forest on the opposite side of the river, then the starlit sky above. "This place speaks to me."

An image flew through his head of keeping Regan secluded in his cabin for weeks or months on end. His hips arched in response. He grabbed for his wine and gulped, then settled in to chow down on the lasagna. He needed this meal.

"You should eat," he said.

"Yes, you're right." She smiled in such a way that he knew she'd caught how much he wanted her right now.

He didn't try to pretend otherwise. He was ready to take her to bed. Only what would it be like, after all these centuries, to be buried between her legs once more?

Chapter Six

What surprised Regan wasn't that Ian was anxious to move things along, but just how clearly she could feel his blood hunger rising. It was like a soft crawl across her skin moving toward her heart. Her own supply had increased and felt like a weight on her chest. Ian needed to feed and she needed a strong bite.

But she also needed nourishment, so she kept her fork busy. "I noticed your cabin has a second smaller story. Is your bedroom up there?"

"No, it's a loft space with a couch and a couple of ottomans as well as a full 360 view."

"Mmmm. Sounds perfect."

He lifted his gaze to her and sipped his wine. Setting the goblet back on the table, he asked, "What do you mean?"

"Well, I already love the view from the deck. To see every possible direction would be heaven."

"Then we should go up there."

"Okay."

When she was done, she offered to clean up and didn't wait for Ian to suggest otherwise. She rose from the table, gathered everything and set to work. She used a soapy sponge to wipe each plate and glass down, as well as the forks. She made quick work of it.

Ian rinsed and dried the dishes, then took her hand. "Come on."

It was definitely time.

He led her to the staircase. She moved quickly up the steps, smiling as she entered the round space. Dark paneling covered the few areas not framed by windows.

The view, just as she'd expected, was magnificent. She took a moment to look out each curved aspect.

Ian waited patiently, though she could feel his tension from across the room. When she reached the last of the windows, completing a full circuit, he drew close, sliding his arms around her from behind.

She leaned her head back and allowed herself to savor this time with him. She couldn't imagine any other circumstance that would have brought them together like this.

She turned in his arms, and he kissed her. She'd always loved the feel of his full lips, which he used to tease her mouth open.

When she parted for him, he slipped his tongue inside and everything shifted. Gone was every concern. In this moment, she felt only Ian and the soft, seductive rhythm as he pulsed within her mouth.

She leaned into him, gripping his arms through his long-sleeved t-shirt, wanting the shirt off, needing to feel her skin against his.

When she drew back, she took the hem and tugged it part way up his chest.

He responded with a smile, and obliged her by pulling the shirt the rest of the way.

She stepped away, eyes wide.

"What?"

"You're magnificent." Her gaze settled on his thick pecs and the hawk tattoo spanning his chest. She took her time exploring each feather etched in black ink and the muscles that lay beneath.

He brought his arms in front of his abdomen, crossing his wrists and flexed each of his muscles for her.

She planted her hands on him, feeling him up, enjoying his hard nipples. "More," she whispered.

He flexed slowly, building up the girth of the muscles, then released.

She dipped and took a nipple in her mouth and as much surrounding flesh as she could reach.

Do it again, she pathed.

She groaned as he flexed. She sucked him, while covering his other nipple with her hand and playing with him.

She drew back, looking at him. She could feel how swollen her lips had become.

"You always enjoyed my body," he said, his gray eyes dark with desire.

She dipped a hand and caressed his arousal. "Yes. Always." She searched his eyes. "You need to feed, don't you?"

He nodded. "But I can wait. It's not like before, like I was always close to falling into a coma."

She caressed his arm, sliding her hand along the line of his shoulder, all the way to his fingers, touching the blood tattoos at the same time. She knew now that the long stripes had become permanent.

She took his hand and pressed it between her breasts. "Can you feel my heart? It's heavy with volume. I'd heard about this, how much extra sustenance a blood rose could create for her man, but now I'm acutely aware. I need to feed you. There's just one thing."

He narrowed his gaze. "What?"

She took the same hand and ran it down her body to the top of her thigh. "I want you drinking from me here. Remember how you used to do it?"

He leaned close to her, the intake of his breath a cool draw against her skin. "Goddess, yes. I loved doing that to you. Hot as hell."

She kissed his forehead, his temple, and down the line of his cheek. "Do it now."

He slid his arms around her then picked her up. Carrying her to the couch, he knocked his knee against the ottoman, pushing it up to meld with the sofa cushions. Laying her on top of the joined pieces of furniture, he knelt in front of her legs, then worked the button above her zipper.

He took his time, leaning down to push her sweater up then kissing her stomach.

Her body rolled beneath the feel of his lips and his fingers now unzipping her pants. He removed her ankle boots first, afterward sliding the pants off one leg at a time. Somewhere in the mix, her thong disappeared.

He spread her legs so that she was fully exposed to him, then stood up and got rid of his own jeans and shoes, his gaze fixed to her bare sex. She took the moment to slide her sweater over her head though she kept her bra on. The underwire pushed her breasts up, and she wanted him looking there as well.

Caris Roane

She leaned up on her elbows, watching his gaze move over her body from her thighs, her sex, her navel and finally her breasts. He groaned as he dropped once more between her legs. Only this time, he put both his hands on her breasts, taking his time to enjoy her the way she'd savored him.

She could feel his rings, which added another layer of sensation. And his scent was rich in her nose, the earthy, forest-fern redolence causing her to clench.

He leaned down and kissed the mounds of her breasts, then dipped a tongue between her skin and her bra, pushing until he found a nipple. He flicked the tight bud over and over. Using his hand, he squeezed her other breast. The dual sensation had her moaning.

She wrapped her legs around his waist, her hips arching as she tried to make contact. She needed the pressure, the sweet feel of his body against her sex.

Using his finger, he slid the fabric of her bra beneath each breast, exposing her. He sucked her nipples, taking turns flicking and laving until her hips rocked. "Ian, you're killing me."

Good, he pathed, sucking harder.

She didn't think she could take much more, when suddenly, he added a vibration to his lips and she cried out. "I could come like this."

Then come. As he sucked her breast, he pressed his abdomen against her sex, pulsing. She tightened her legs and ecstasy began to flow, a soft series of explosions deep inside her well. She cried out long and loud.

The whole time, he ground against her, sustaining the intense pleasure.

When the wave passed and her body began to settle, he released her breast, placing tender kisses on each beaded nipple.

"You have the most beautiful breasts."

She pushed his damp hair behind his ear. "Thank you. And you've always known how to bring me."

He rose up a little. "Now arch your back because I want your bra off."

She did as he commanded and while kissing her, he reached behind her to unclasp her bra. He dragged it away from her breasts and tossed it on top of the rest of their clothes.

As he began to kiss his way down her abdomen, her heart started to pound because she knew what was coming. He opened his mouth and rubbed back and forth, letting her feel the sides of his fangs.

The vampire needed to feed.

"Ian. Yes."

He tongued her navel, swirling and pressing. She clenched again and desire once more flowed through her, sending shivers over her stomach and deep between her legs.

When he reached her sex, he slid his arms beneath her legs and began to lick, long swipes of his tongue starting at her opening then moving over the sensitive folds. He repeated the process slowly, at times dipping into her well before continuing up.

Her hips rocked, pushing her sex into his face. His hands gripped her firmly, the feel of his rings once more adding to her pleasure. She was breathing hard all over again. "Ian, what you're doing to me—"

I know your body, Regan. I remember everything, and I want you to come again. How about this? When a new vibration left his tongue, she groaned heavily as pleasure raced up her well. The same sensation then traveled across her sex as he pressed his tongue against her and kept adding to the frequency. Faster the vibration went.

Her hips were jumping off the ottoman and once more, ecstasy exploded through her body, his vibrating tongue working magic that no other lover had been able to achieve.

The strange image went through her head of bringing Ian into her fae retreat, then chaining him to her bed for a decade or two. Maybe a century.

He sustained the vibration until again her body grew lax.

I'm so hungry for you, he pathed. The vibration had disappeared from his tongue as he moved to her upper thigh.

He began licking above her vein in heavy strokes. Taking blood from the groin wasn't for amateurs. But she was confident in Ian; he knew what he was doing. He'd supped from her this way all those centuries ago.

Knowing how pleasurable it would be to feel his fangs, she couldn't keep her hips still. With a need to prevent her from getting injured, Ian overlaid her abdomen with his arm, pinning her in place.

She could feel her vein rising, coming to the surface, obedient to the vampire. She arched her neck, her eyes closed as she focused on the sensation of having him bite her as he prepared to drink from her.

Once more, her heart pounded, ready to serve.

Shall I pierce your vein?

Yes, please, yes. I need this, Ian. Now.

She panted, anticipating.

Embrace the Hunt

The next moment he struck and she cried out as her well clenched. A small explosion darted through her, a sort of mini-orgasm giving her skin a new flush of pleasure.

Ian began to drink and the sound of his suckling mouth had her panting in light wisps of air.

Using his free hand, he found her well and slid two fingers inside. *Is this what you need? I've never heard you sound so desperate.*

I'm almost out of my mind. I can't get enough. He drove his fingers in and out. She felt her well relax then tighten. All the sensations together, his rings hitting her sex, the sound and feel of his suckling as he took her blood down his throat, and the plunging of his hand, took her straight up to the pinnacle yet again.

She came screaming, her body on fire with pleasure.

~ ~ ~

Ian didn't know which was making him harder, Regan's screams as he drove his fingers in and out of her or the powerful nature of her blood.

I need to fuck you, Regan.

She groaned at his words. *Ian, I need your cock, too. I need you deep, hard, and fast.*

I'm not done drinking.

Seal me up, then take the vein at my throat. Please, Ian. I want you inside me.

He didn't need to be begged twice. Using his tongue, he swiped over the punctures at her groin, stopping the flow of blood.

He rose, and taking his cock in hand, placed the tip at her well and began to push. She was so wet and he was hard as hell.

Lying with her bottom on the ottoman and her back on the middle of the couch, she wrapped her legs once more around his hips. She rolled her head to the side and pushed her hair away from her throat. Very ready.

Once he was seated inside her, he licked her neck. He thought he might have to wait for the vein to rise, but it was already there. His fangs dripped with saliva as he angled, preparing to bite. His chin trembled as he struck and her blood once more began to flow.

When he formed a seal and began to suck, he set up a steady rhythm with his hips, driving deep.

Yes, Ian. Another heavy moan followed.

He'd never been so turned on in his life. Or powered up. *Your blood, Regan, is like a fire in me. Feel my arms.*

Though her head was turned to the side, she reached up and grabbed his arm with her right hand, her fingers pressing into his muscles. *Ian, you're bigger, which I didn't think was possible. What's happening?*

You're doing this, because you're a blood rose.

When he moved faster, she writhed beneath him, moaning. He focused on his cock and added a serious vibration. He barely recognized the heavy sound that came from her throat, half grunt, half moan and he loved it.

He also knew she was once more close to orgasm and the feel of her tight pulsing well caused his balls to draw up, getting ready.

He drew back from her vein, swiping the wounds once more. She shifted her head back so she could look at him. For a split-second, all he saw was her and how much he'd always desired her and craved her. His chest swelled with so much feeling that for a moment he felt lost.

"Ian," she said, her jasmine-lime scent now perfuming the space between them.

He came back to himself, his body ready for release. He moved his hips faster, wanting to watch her writhe with another orgasm as he drove to the finish. "Can you come again? Come with me?"

She nodded, her lips parted, her breathing erratic. Tears filled her eyes and he felt her clench low. His cock was hard, so hard, then he began to release. He got lost in the intensity of the pleasure, the fiery sensations pulsing the length of his cock over and over.

He could feel Regan bucking against him and he heard her screaming so he knew they were sharing the moment. Her face was flushed, her neck arched, her lips parted.

As his orgasm subsided, he felt very strange as though he wasn't finished. He knew then he was gearing up for a second round. "Holy fucking shit. Regan, look at me."

She opened her eyes. She was gasping for breath. "What?"

He pumped his hips a few times to let her feel.

Her doe eyes widened. "Oh, sweet Goddess, you're still hard."

"I am and I'm going to give it to you again."

Her voice hit a deeper register as she gripped his arms, her hips rolling to meet his. "Yes. Give it to me. Fast."

He sped up, driving into her as fast as he could, pistoning in and out of her.

Her body grew flushed again as once more throaty cries left her lips. His balls released, shooting more pulses of intense sensation through his cock. He roared his pleasure, over and over until he'd spent his seed.

She clung to him as his body settled down. She was panting and laughing. "That was amazing."

"It was." He breathed hard, stunned by the double release. "I've never done that before." He smiled down at her. "You have, though. You're just as I remember you, very sensual for such a spiritual being."

She stroked her hand down his neck and across his shoulder. "Is that how you see me?"

"Exactly."

"And I see you as a leader of men, a warrior, incredibly built in every way." Here she dipped her hips enough to feel the length of him.

There was so much feel-good drifting through his veins, he couldn't help but smile.

"But there's something more." She squeezed his shoulder. "I value your service to the Nine Realms above all else. Your work with both your Vampire Guard and Shifter Brigade has set the standard for other realms. You've saved lives."

He stared down at her and a frown split his brow as he remembered the past. "But not enough lives."

"You're too hard on yourself, Ian. You always were."

"And I didn't cut you any slack either, did I?"

She shook her head.

He was still buried inside her as the old issues came up. Yet, somehow, he didn't want to keep thinking the same thoughts. Had he been wrong about her? What if she hadn't enthralled him? What if something else had been at work that night? Only what?

Slowly, he drew out of her.

She flung an arm over her head, watching him. "It's okay, Ian. I'm not here to change your opinion of what happened so long ago. And I know we're in a weird place. We've been thrown together in this really bizarre way. The benefits so far have been amazing, but I'm not naïve; the sharing of blood and sex will not fix what's wrong between us.

"In the meantime, I want to be in your bed, if you can handle it, to be as close to you as I can. My fae instincts tell me whatever this is between us will affect the fate of the Nine Realms. More than anything, I want to help end this war."

He nodded, turning to grab his t-shirt off the stack of clothes. He wadded it up and tucked it between her legs. He'd left a lot of himself behind.

"Thanks," she murmured.

"I'm not backing away, Regan. I need you to know that. I have my concerns just as you do. But Camberlaune comes first. So, yes, you'll be sharing my bed. Stone believes we're meant to accomplish something together. And if he's right, I don't want to make a serious mistake by failing to engage with your blood rose ability."

"I'm with you, Ian. All the way. I love our world and I've hated what Margetta has done to it. Whatever we have to do, I'm in." She leaned up on her elbows and smiled. "But right now, I'd love another shower."

He chuckled. "You got it." He rose to his feet, then picked her up, intent on carrying her to the bathroom downstairs.

She wrapped her arms around his neck, sighing at the same time. "The sex was wonderful, Ian."

"Yes, it was." He knew he sounded very male, but it had been awesome.

~ ~ ~

Regan loved that Ian carried her down to the first floor. This was one of the reasons she'd fallen so hard for him all those years ago. He was attentive in unexpected ways.

His bedroom overlooked the deep woods behind the house, as did a massive open shower with several heads.

He turned them on, but instead of leaving her on her own, he stayed and took his time soaping her. Again, unexpected, which warmed her heart.

When they'd been together previously, Ian had taken a lot of pleasure in her body in the same way she'd pretty much worshiped his. Still, she knew his mindset. Yet his willingness to shower with her made her almost hopeful.

When he asked her to spread her legs with a voice that had dropped a couple of timbres, she slung an arm around his neck and kissed him. A few minutes later, she was pinned to the bathroom tile, her legs once more wrapped around his hips as he pounded into her.

Later, and tucked between the sheets, she began to drift off. But her last thought jarred her back awake: Could their shared power help her to create a spell that would penetrate and dissolve Margetta's shielding mist?

She was about to wake Ian up to talk it over with him. But he lay on his back, an arm over his eyes and she decided to let the matter rest until they each got some sleep.

When she woke up, a dim distant light around the outdoor shutters told her it was late afternoon. She turned on her side to face into the room and had a view of Ian's bare knees, heavily muscled legs, and black boxers. Two hands held a coffee cup. For a moment, her gaze rested on all the rings he wore, ten heavy pieces of man-jewelry, each different.

She lifted her eyes to the rest of the man. He sat in a heavy wood chair next to the bed, watching her with a crooked smile on his lips.

"Hey," he said quietly. He must have remembered she didn't like loud voices when she first woke up.

She immediately reached for her hair and stroked a couple of times. She was sure she had a terrible case of bed-head, but Ian didn't seem to mind. She glanced at the cup. "You made coffee?"

"I did." He gestured to the night stand. "Yours is right there if you want it."

She made a cooing sound. "Just what I need."

She pulled the sheet and blanket up around her and scooted to a sitting position. Holding the covers in place, she jammed one of the pillows behind her back.

She took the warm mug in both hands and cradled it. Eyes closed, she sipped then let out a long, deep sigh.

"I've always loved that about you."

"What?" She popped her eyes open. "That I like coffee?"

He shook his head. "No, that you're sensual in your physical reactions to everything." A wave of forest-fern scent rolled over her, sending a new shiver of desire racing through her.

She sipped again, staring at him over the rim of her mug. Ian wore nothing but boxers which set his broad shoulders and chest on display. It would take so little to encourage him to come back to bed, and she almost crooked her finger and extended the invitation. But she wanted to talk about how they'd shared their power during the attack at his home and about the possibility that together they could find a way to dispel the mist.

Unfortunately, her gaze fell to the tattoo of the hawk spanning his chest, her eye drawn to his thick pecs. A flush crept up her cheeks. Ian was all man and everything about him got to her.

She had to look away. Otherwise, in about two seconds, she was going to throw the covers back and doing some serious begging.

"O-k-a-y." She blinked a few times and drew a ragged breath or two.

Ian left his chair, however, to sit on the side of the bed next to her. His eyes were at half-mast. "Do you need me? Because I'm here if you do."

Her gaze flipped to his and her heartrate rose. She realized she'd already started developing a now familiar sensation in her chest, the weight of an increased supply meant for him. Her lips parted. She was so tempted, but she had more important things on her mind.

Forcing herself to the matter at hand, she said, "Ian, we should talk about Margetta."

He chuckled. "Well, if that isn't a buzz-kill."

Some of the tension left her and she rushed on. "As I was falling asleep last night, I was thinking about what happened in your home, when we battled Braden and his bonded wraith. You'd never experienced such a surge of power before and I couldn't believe I actually levitated to head-kick a mastyr vampire."

"Wait. Is that what happened?"

She nodded. "Yes. He was real close to taking you out. I had to do something."

"You saved my life then."

"As you did mine."

He shook his head. "I didn't know what had happened to make Braden stop. He was kicking my spine. I thought I was done for."

"You were almost unconscious by then. But my blood tattoos were alive and I'd never felt so ramped up in my life. You told me to go with my instincts, so I did."

He frowned hard, but said nothing.

"What?" she asked.

"I'm replaying the battle with Braden. He had so much power in every blow."

"I've heard when a mastyr completes the Invictus bond with a wraith, they're undefeatable in a one-on-one. He was so confident he could take you. But we'd both be dead if he'd brought in a couple of wraith-pairs to back him up."

His jaw worked. "You're right. We got lucky, which is why I brought you here. Only one person knows the location of this cabin."

"Ben?"

"No, not even Ben. Only my property caretaker."

"Right. The one whose wife made the lasagna."

"Yep." He brought his mug to his lips and drank, but his frown remained. He was thinking hard.

He was such a gorgeous man and had the most beautiful eyes, an unusual dark gray with thick black lashes. His long hair hung down his back, inviting her fingers to do some touching.

Instead, she sipped her coffee and once more forced herself to look away. She'd sort of hoped the lovemaking the night before, including the surprising round in the shower, would have eased her desire for him. Instead, it seemed to have fanned the flame; she wanted him more than ever.

She needed to focus and turned her thoughts to her blood tattoos. "What if together we could enhance my spell-making ability enough to counter Margetta's spell?"

He leaned forward, holding his cup in both hands between his knees. "How would that work? I mean, I'm about as far from fae abilities as anyone can get. I've never understood how you people do what you do. I know that you de-spelled the shield around the Swanicott camp out at Angler's Cliff, but I can't fathom the process."

"How much do you want to know?"

"What it's like. The steps you take. That sort of thing. Maybe if I had an idea what was involved, I'd see a way to make it work."

"Okay." She thought for a moment. "Well, first and most importantly, I meditate, especially when it comes to countering a spell or if I'm trying to fashion a new spell. I remember when I was working on Margetta's spell in Swanicott, I spent two hours in deep meditation. But toward the end, the counter-spell came to me like a poem. It was amazing and very spiritual."

"And no amount of meditation worked while you were held captive in Margetta's tower."

She shook her head slowly, remembering. "You have no idea how hard I tried. But it felt as though because I'd worked out the counter-spell for the Angler's Cliff camp, Margetta had used that to strengthen her spell around her fortress."

He narrowed his eyes. "That doesn't make sense."

"Every spell has a signature as did my counter-spell. To some degree, because I'd worked out the counter-spell, I should know Margetta's sequence better. Instead she'd read my Swanicott counter-spell and I'm convinced she found a way to block me. At least, that's my conclusion at this point. But … "

He waited. "Finish your thought."

"I believe we could get rid of the block, if we worked together, you and me. Would you be willing to try?"

"Of course, if you think it would help. But I'm a vampire. I don't see how I'll be much use."

"I don't need you to bring certain abilities to the table, if that's your concern, just your power and how we are together, how our power flares when we touch." She reached toward him and overlaid the blood tattoos of his left arm with her hand.

She caught her breath as a surge of power warmed her palm and flowed up her arm. She met his gaze. "Want to give it a shot right now?"

"Sure. Why not?"

"Good." She set her mug down and leaned back against the pillow. Closing her eyes, she kept the power flowing and dropped into her meditative state. She could feel that Ian stayed with her. He didn't move or his shift his arm in any way, but remained sitting on the bed.

What do you need me to do? he asked.

Keep the power flowing just as you are.

But I'm not doing anything.

She smiled. *Then keep doing that.*

His deep chuckle flowed through the room.

Knowing Ian was with her completely, she relaxed even more and let herself fall deeper still into what was a highly vulnerable state. Her surroundings disappeared so that soon she felt as though she was floating.

Her inner senses came alive as they never had before. She'd always had an internal palette from which she worked, a variety of colors, words, and symbols she would fashion when constructing a spell, even musical patterns.

Counter-spells were much more complicated to create especially since among her fae community, such incantations were rarely ever needed. Sometimes one of her novices would require her help. But at such an elemental level, she barely had to dip into her meditation to fashion the necessary corrective process.

This time, she floated within her mind, every cell of her body centered on Margetta's mist spell and the block she had in place. Almost immediately, however, a black cloud began to descend within her mind. She gripped Ian's arm and felt him respond by tightening his own. The blood tattoos heated up even more, warming her skin and expanding the shared power.

She brought that same power deep into her mind, fighting against what felt very familiar, as though Margetta was actually with her.

But Regan knew the black cloud was just a blocking spell. Much about being fae at Regan's level involved staying with the hunt for the right sequence of elements, keeping focused. She only had to find the key to Margetta's signature and she'd be able to destroy the spell.

As Regan faced the black cloud, she held the shared power steady. She directed all her thoughts and senses to the structure of the blocking spell, yet she couldn't pin it down or in any way find its formula.

Ian, I'm so close but I need more from you, if you can possibly help.

Tell me what to do and I'll do it. Though I have to say you're emitting tremendous energy. You're red aura is glowing all around your body and your blood tattoos are pulsing in a dark burgundy hue.

Her aura was the reason she was known as the Ruby Fae. From the time she could remember, whenever she connected in a strong way with her fae power, she gave off a red shimmering light.

She kept her eyes closed and explored the images within the blocking spell and an idea came to her. *Take both my arms, but this time engage your battle energy. The blocking spell that's preventing me from understanding Margetta's mist creation is in front of me. I want to see if by using your strongest energy I can finally figure the spell out.*

Will do. What a comfort his deep resonant voice was even inside her mind.

She kept her eyes shut and felt the bed shift. Ian never lost touch as he maneuvered so that he could take both her hands in his.

The moment the circle was complete and he began to access his battle vibration, her blood tattoos turned hot, her neck arched, and a fiery power flowed through her.

With such tremendous support, Regan let the black cloud infuse her mind. She was deep in her meditation now and she'd lost all sense of time passing.

With Ian's power moving through her, she was able to set the cloud spinning slowly. Every particle of Regan's fae being kept touching the spell, pondering, examining, sensing.

Once the entire spell made a complete circuit, Margetta's pattern began to emerge. Finally, as though a key turned in a lock, the secret to the blocking spell opened to her with a sequence of words, colors, and melodies.

She wanted to cry out in triumph, but feared losing the moment. Instead, by making use of the components of the dark spell, she created a counter-spell. Taking a deep breath, she let it fly.

The effect was immediate. The black cloud began to thin and fade to a grayish hue. Finally, it dissipated, vanishing completely. In response, Regan's mind grew light and airy, her spirit free.

She'd broken the block.

Have you done it, Regan, because I'm sensing a big change.

Yes, the blocking spell is completely gone. But we did it together. I couldn't have penetrated the formula for the spell without your power. However, I can't stop now. This is only half of what needs to be accomplished.

You intend to work on the shielding mist itself? He asked.

Yes. I think with your support, I'll be able to analyze the mist spell without having to be at the gorge. So, stay with me. Okay?

Go for it. I'm here.

Knowing he was still with her, helped Regan to set all her attention on the mist-spell. She'd studied the camp portion of the spell thoroughly during her time in the fortress. Though she'd never been able to do anything about it, she'd imprinted it on her mind and brought it forward now.

The moment she brought it to life, she knew it was the same spell that had caused the mist, though she hadn't seen the mist until she'd actually left the tower. This was a huge relief, since she'd only be dealing with one spell.

Yet, how different the spell appeared because the blocking portion was gone. Everything had been jumbled before. Now the colors were more vibrant, the melodies clearer, and even the incantations made sense.

As the spell's structure began to emerge, she realized she was looking not at a simple, single spell, but one with a series of intricate layers. This was her first real clue as to how to break it down.

Ian, I'm able to see the spell in its entirety. It's amazingly intricate, with layers, which is one reason I could never comprehend it before.

Not sure I know what you mean, but I can feel your excitement. What's next?

It's pretty simple; all I have to do is uncover the structure of the first layer then the rest will follow.

Can you do that now?

I'm pretty sure I can.

Then keep going.

More time passed as she remained in meditation. Every fae instinct told her to stay with it, to not let any aspect of the spell slip through the open weave of her thoughts.

Images of Margetta's mist swirled in front of her, a haunting collection of words, colors and carefully chosen melodic sequences. What she saw and felt was incredibly beautiful, even seductive.

Whatever else Margetta might be, she was a lovely creature to behold, both physically and in her fae abilities. Regan wondered what had happened in Margetta's life to have taken her down such a dark, destructive path. When had she chosen a life of domination rather than one of service?

Margetta was very old and Regan knew next to nothing about her early centuries. Perhaps some catastrophe had occurred in her life to alter forever a desire to do good. Regan would likely never know.

Now, of course, all that truly mattered was defeating her.

As the images moved in swift circles now, the structure of a complex counter-spell at last emerged.

She laid it within her consciousness, so that she'd always know its exact sequence and composition.

With everything in place, she left her meditation and opened her eyes.

A soft wind full of magic and power blew through the bedroom so that Ian's hair was lifted away from his face. His golden skin was flushed, his muscles pumped, and a sheen of sweat covered his body.

"Ian, you look so different."

"And you have the most beautiful red aura. Whatever this is between us, Regan, power is what we create together. And for that, I'm grateful. I'm convinced we'll be able to do this thing."

Here was the man she'd always loved. Those feelings had never stopped and she knew she'd compared every man she'd ever dated to Ian. In many ways, she should have been drawn to a sensitive fae artist or teacher. Instead, only a warrior would do and not just any, but the Mastyr of Camberlaune.

"I need you to take me back to the area of the gorge near the fortress," she said. "I wasn't able to see beyond the first layer and I think I need to be present with the mist to construct each sequence."

Slowly, he drew his hands away from her. The sensation made her smile, because it felt like the connection was made of taffy, giving a strange tug as he let go. When he no longer touched her, the shared power faded quickly then disappeared.

His gaze swept from one shoulder up and over her head then down the other side. "Your red glow has disappeared."

She nodded. "And the breeze in the room is gone." She settled against the pillows, becoming aware she was still naked in bed.

But something had changed. She glanced at the windows. The shutters were fully retracted and the forest was dark. She searched her internal clock and realized with a start how much time had passed.

Shifting her gaze back to Ian, her eyes widened. "Was I really meditating for two hours?"

He nodded. "You were."

"I barely had an awareness of time passing."

"No worries, Regan. I could sense it was important for you to keep going. And as soon as we've had a proper meal, I'll take you to the fortress."

"Maybe we should go now."

But he shook his head. "Trust me in this. We both need to eat first because I have a feeling we're facing another long night."

Chapter Seven

Once he'd shared a substantial meal with Regan, of scrambled eggs, sausage, and thick slices of toasted cottage bread, he prepared for the night. While she showered, he contacted Ben to see how active the Invictus were.

Fortunately, they'd concentrated their efforts in the far eastern reaches of his realm, a place near the smaller Venaset Mountain range dominated by his Shifter Brigade. Stone was already in the region and helped to direct both the Brigade and his Vampire Guard from village to village as the wraith-pairs attacked.

He chose not to tell either Stone or Ben about what was going on with Regan. Some instinct warned him he should protect their purpose, at least for now. Besides, until they actually had an effect on the mist there was nothing to tell.

He showered in the guest room and put on his Guard uniform, minus the woven shirt. When he'd gotten the hawk tattoo, he'd decided to forgo wearing the shirt. Most of his *doneuses* had made a lot of noise about the tattoo and for a solid year, he'd had more sex because of it than any previous time. And he'd never lacked.

Regan had spread her fingers over each of the feathers, then felt up his pecs and sucked on him.

Though he'd been with a lot of women, out of all of them, Regan had his number. He couldn't explain it, and this had been true long before the whole blood rose thing, but she made him feel things no other woman could. Which meant that anytime a date of his reminded him of Regan, even in the smallest way, the comparison began. Invariably, the woman fell short.

If he actually believed in soulmates, he'd say Regan was it.

Except that he didn't trust her. He couldn't. She'd let him down by keeping him with her when he should have been out battling. And he couldn't forgive her because of all the lives lost.

When she emerged from the bedroom, he saw that she'd swept her light brown hair away from her face which emphasized her strong cheekbones. Her beauty struck him all over again, causing his heart to squeeze up tight once more. Her large brown eyes widened as she looked him up and down.

She smiled. "Love you without the shirt, Ian. Between the tattoo and the black leather of your sleeveless coat … wow."

His gaze drifted down her skintight jeans and black ankle boots. He knew the shapes of those legs, and what they'd felt like wrapped around his hips as he drove into her.

He felt in danger of falling for her all over again, and part of him resented her for it. Despite that she'd had about as much control in their current blood rose situation as he had, he still wished he wasn't getting all tangled up again. Except, damn the sex had been good.

"I need to say something." He planted his fists on his hips, his rings making a clinking sound. "Just to be clear, my feelings toward you haven't changed."

She shrugged. "I know." Could she have been more matter of fact?

He scowled. "You almost sound as though you don't care."

She tilted her head. "Ian, I know we have serious issues between us so believe me, I have no expectations here. And even if you suddenly had a change of heart, I'm not sure I'd believe you or be able to trust you."

"What do you mean by that?" He was irritated because he'd never given her a reason not to trust him.

"Ian, you broke my heart. I don't think I could go through that again. What we have here because I'm a blood rose is nothing short of amazing. But I know it can't last, and I'm willing to go along for the ride because I'm convinced we'll be able to do some good together. But I definitely don't see this as you and me forging a life together. I think it's a lovely, sexy interlude, that's all."

He was dumbfounded as he frowned at her. "There are so many things wrong with what you've said, I don't know where to begin. For one thing, you speak as though it will be a simple thing for you to walk away once we've gotten the mist situation resolved. But it won't be."

He'd never seen her look more serious as she responded. "You're wrong. For me, it will be easy. What was hard, was living with your attitude toward me for the past five centuries. I didn't deserve it, Ian. As I see it, you fell into a whole lot of guilt because of Raven's Overlook and you took it out on me."

He shook his head, stunned she held these opinions. For a brief second, he wondered if she was right. Had his guilt clouded his perception? Whatever the case, he'd never be able to make her see where she was at fault, so for now he had to let it go. "I don't want to quarrel with you. We each see the past very differently. We should go, though right now I'm pretty pissed."

She huffed a sigh. "And just for the record, Ian, the only thing I was ever guilty of that night was loving you to the point of madness. Now, let's get going. I have a counter-spell living like wildfire inside me, and I'm ready to take down some mist."

"Fine."

She lifted one arched brow. "Fine."

Once in the air, Ian's temper started to cool. Flying helped. Sweet Goddess, he loved to be in the air. His blood tattoos had lit up the moment she'd wrapped an arm around his neck. He flew faster than ever with Regan's power flowing over him.

She'd fallen silent, having had her say. She didn't even attempt to communicate telepathically. But she held onto his neck, even though he had her pinned to his side with an arm around her waist. It was funny how at peace she seemed to be in their impossible situation.

She'd said she'd loved him to the point of madness. He'd heard the expression before and he had to admit he'd been crazy in love with her back then as well. But she'd enthralled him, whatever she chose to believe. Even Ben had said he'd seen it from the first, that Regan had somehow used her fae abilities to keep him close.

The massacre had changed everything in his life. From that point forward, he'd never taken relationships with women seriously; he couldn't afford to.

~ ~ ~

Regan kept her cool, but something about Ian's continued insistence she'd enthralled him had started tearing at her heart. She wasn't mad; she knew his opinion. But she'd never stopped loving him, and now that she was so physically close to him again, her love had started rising to the surface once more.

She'd meant what she'd said. She really didn't have a single damn expectation of him. But all the closeness of the night before and even this evening with his power supporting her meditations, had started smashing down her careful walls. She didn't want to be feeling so much for him because the end game hadn't changed. However, this terrible middle place of extreme proximity and satisfying sex had her heart aching.

In fact, she hurt so deep she could hardly breathe, though she worked hard at appearing impassive. She forced her lungs to expand and air to flow back in.

Ian moved swiftly through the night sky, but he didn't follow the foothills this time. Instead, he flew over the mountains, heading toward Dark Gorge. She could sense the trajectory with her innate Realm homing ability.

When he began his descent, he was once more almost at the border between Camberlaune and Tannisford Realm. She saw the long wall of mist as barely a line at first, but growing in mass as they drew closer to the land.

She was reminded forcefully of her recent incarceration and the ways Margetta had tortured her. She shuddered.

You okay?

Just remembering. Don't worry. I'll get over it.

I know you will. But we need to have a plan ready in case any Invictus pairs show up. I'd be a fool to try to do battle right now. So I'm thinking that while you do your thing, I'll keep watch. But I reserve the right to take off fast the moment the enemy shows up. Agreed?

She had no problem with his plan. *Any sign of those devils, even if I'm in the middle of stripping the first layer of mist away, you get us out of there.*

Good.

Near the gorge, Ian descended to the stretch of granite that created a precipice overlooking the thousand foot drop below. The moment he landed, she stepped off his booted foot and turned toward the mist. Time to forget her troubles and face the much more important task ahead of her.

Because she'd figured out the mist's complex, layered structure, she saw it in a new way.

Hey, he pathed. When she turned to meet his gaze, she saw the concerned look in his eye. *Sorry we got into.*

She shook her head. *Don't give it a second thought. I don't believe it's ever a bad thing to speak your mind.* She turned toward the mist once more. *Now let's see what we can do to start unraveling Margetta's spell.*

Where do you want me?

I'm going to need your physical support because I'll be meditating as I do this. So, stand behind me, then reach around and put your hands on my blood tattoos.

When he drew near, she lifted her arms. He moved in close, straddling her feet with his boots. When he slid his fingers down her arms and covered her tattoos, she shivered as much from his touch as from the sudden vibration of power.

Damn this is amazing.

Magical, she pathed softly.

And it was, like nothing she'd ever experienced, especially because he supported her from behind. She felt as though she could do anything.

I'm going into my meditation now, so I won't be fully present. Does that make sense?

Don't worry, Regan. I've got you. But be prepared that if I see a wraith-pair, I'll sweep you into the skies.

I understand. And now, here I go.

Not knowing how long the process would take, she folded their joined arms across her stomach. He moved with her so that essentially he was embracing her. The intimacy about killed her, but she had to let it go.

Taking a deep breath, she refocused her attention on the mist.

She closed her eyes and drew the counter-spell forward in her mind, the colors and melodic lines, the words. Turning her hands palms up, she let the spell became a vibration, flowing through her mind and her body. When the spell-breaking energy reached her arms, she felt Ian's power gather as well and suddenly infuse the vibration.

That's it, Ian. Now keep your hands loose over me, but retain contact. And follow my lead.

I will and right now I can sense the counter-spell building inside you.

I'll only be taking out a small portion of the layer right in front of us to make sure the spell works. If or when it does, we can decide how we want to proceed.

She felt Ian take a deep breath. *That's an excellent strategy which will keep our efforts here quiet for now.*

I think so, too.

She slowly opened her fingers and began to spread her arms wide. Ian stayed with her, gliding his hands along her arms as she moved, sustaining contact.

The power built until she knew the exact moment she needed to release.

Now, she whispered from her mind to his.

The counter-spell synced with their combined powers. The blood tattoos pulsed on her skin and she could feel an answering vibration in his.

The spell released, a heavy wave of energy heading straight for the massive wall of mist. It caught the initial layer and began spinning the mist, twisting it into small cyclones that rose in the air then faded into vapor.

Because it was only a small section of the first layer, what remained was a shallow area with much less dense mist. Yet, Regan could see shapes moving within.

Ian, I think I'm seeing wraith-pairs. Will they attack us?

I see movement as well, but I'm not sure we're in any danger. Because the mist creates a shielding disguise both directions, they probably can't see us. He dropped his hands from her arms, moving past her, but she kept pace with him. He stopped when the moving shapes became clearer, though still mist-disguised.

Ian was right. They weren't under attack. Instead, they were seeing the edge of the army encampment. But not a single-wraith-pair turned in their direction.

Ian pathed, *How soon do you think you can create the remaining counter-spells?*

Very quickly. A matter of only seconds per layer. What we've done over the past few minutes has provided a signature base from which to work. It's ingrained within my consciousness now.

~ ~ ~

Ian knew exactly what needed to be done.
We're going to fly.

He turned to her, holding out his arm. She quickly climbed up on his foot, and he drew her tight against him.

He rose into the air straight up, rocket fast, then turned to head east to the plain.

His head whirred with a very specific idea. He almost contacted Stone, but something held him back. Same with Ben. What needed to be done had to be kept secret.

As he passed the rim cliffs, he slowed because he had to think. He had an opportunity to change the course of the war right now, but his instincts shouted at him that he needed to be smart about it, maybe even deceptive.

If Margetta's fortress had existed between Camberlaune and Tannisford all this time, then Margetta no doubt had a spy network in place. After battling Braden, Ian had finally been forced to accept the possibility that his Vampire Guard and even his Shifter Brigade had been compromised.

Ian, what's going on? You've slowed.

I'm thinking.

Can I help?

He paused in flight and levitated midair. They were high above a small village, no doubt invisible to anyone who would be looking up.

He held her loosely as she pushed back to gain enough distance to meet his gaze. Though Regan could levitate and fly on her own, Ian was much faster. "What's going on?" she asked. "Something's bugging you. I can feel it."

"I've just realized I don't know who to trust in my combined forces. If Braden could be turned, who I'd always believed had my back despite his ambitions, then others could as well. If I order a full out assault and even one of my vampires or shifters is a spy, the whole operation would be lost."

"And you want to attack now?"

He nodded. "Tonight. We might not be able to destroy the army, but we could do some serious damage. If you peel back the mist as quickly as you say you can, we'll have the element of surprise. And everything you've related about Margetta's attitude tells me an assault is the last thing she would expect."

Her eyes widened, glittering. "So what can I do?"

"Hear me out and give me some feedback. I want to go around the realm over the next few hours and coordinate an attack for three in the morning, well before dawn but with plenty of time for the shifters to get up the mountain.

"I'll deliver orders personally to each squad out in the field with the understanding that I'm sending their group on a secret reconnaissance mission. Using geographical coordinates, each team will be placed at careful intervals at the edge of the mist. The squads won't be able to see the camp, the fortress, or the mist, not until your counter-spell goes into effect."

Regan's brows rose. "So you're saying not even Stone or Ben would know your plans?" She appeared shocked. "But you trust each implicitly."

"I have one goal here. I want to reduce to an absolute minimum the possibility Margetta could ever learn about my plans. Both Stone and Ben have men in the Vampire Guard and the Shifter Brigade they trust. But if any of these have been compromised, I could have a disaster on my hands."

"Okay. I see your thinking. I get it now."

"Tell me what you think, since the plan depends on your ability to roll back the mist at a specific hour. Do you see any holes?

Should I include at least Ben who's been my right hand all these centuries?"

She appeared to consider, her brow furrowing for a long moment. Finally, she drew a deep breath. "I say you go with your instincts. Seeing Braden as part of a wraith-pair has changed my view of things as well. Margetta could have recruited a lot of dissatisfied Realm-folk over the years."

The one thing Ian knew was he trusted Regan in this situation, despite the past. "And you're sure about paring back the mist?"

"I have no doubt it can be done and very quickly."

"Is there a chance Margetta will have already realized you've removed a portion of the first layer?"

"A very small one. She would have to be patrolling the section I worked on and I don't see that happening. According to the servants, Margetta rarely left the fortress itself. She spent most of her time either with her husband, Gustave, or working in her chambers below ground. Although, there was some talk she'd built a communication network similar to your centers, one in each realm."

At that, Ian scowled. "Are you saying somewhere in Camberlaune, the woman operates a center of her own?"

"I think so, but I don't know how sophisticated her system would be. Remember, this was fortress gossip."

Of everything Ian had ever heard about Margetta, including her ability to organize the Invictus into a fighting army, centers of operation in each realm disturbed him. Margetta had tremendous natural powers and all the fae gifts including mist-making spells and enthrallment. But these alone wouldn't command the Nine Realms as a whole. Communication centers, however, were a different matter and spoke to the woman's long-view.

"Sweet Goddess." He felt his heartbeat drumming in his neck. Now was the time to do battle against the woman's ruthless ambitions. He'd never been more certain of anything in his life or more confident in the nature of his plans.

Regan was right to tell him to trust his gut. Everything she'd said supported both his timing and the way he wanted to handle the upcoming engagement.

His battle energy vibrated down his arms, ready to explode from his hands. He needed to dial it down, but a sense of urgency was on him.

He drew Regan close to his side once more and contacted Ben telepathically.

Hey, Ben responded. *Good to hear from you. Everything okay?*

Yes, absolutely. Then he concocted his lie. *I have Regan with me and we've been working the mist but not having a lot of success yet. Regan will keep trying. Are you at the Communication Center?*

I am.

How's the Invictus activity so far?

Very low, but I have squads scattered all over the realm.

These were Ian's standard orders. *Good. Excellent.*

What's going on, Ian? You seem different.

Shit. A minute out of the gate and already Ben could tell something was up. He wasn't much for dissimulation anyway.

For another few seconds, he debated bringing Ben in on his plans. He trusted Ben with his life. He always would.

But given he was in the Communication Center with a number of ears ready to listen in, Ian retreated back to his original intention of keeping his plans hidden from everyone.

Answering Ben's question, he said, *It's having a blood rose. I'm revved up because I'm out of pain.*

I can only imagine. Ben was a mastyr and had lived for almost as many centuries as Ian with chronic blood starvation and the accompanying constant discomfort.

Are the troops out at the usual locations?

By the book.

Ian began to breathe a little easier. He wouldn't have to hunt his men down; he knew where the squads would be. *I'll be roaming the realm tonight with Regan in tow. We'll probably drop down to Winnick for a midnight meal. Other than that, path me if you need me.*

Will do.

He felt Ben end the communication.

Mentally, Ian laid out the same grid of Camberlaune as at the center. Having preset points of arrival and set areas for hunting for Invictus sign would make Ian's job of reaching each squad a much simpler task.

Regan suggested she use her cell to map the misted area and create specific geographical points for each squad. She had strong homing abilities, as he did, so he knew she'd get the coordinates right.

With his plan in place, he headed to the closest region first, which was the long stretch of foothill communities at the base of the Dauphaire Rim. The Rim was the place where the mountains dropped five-hundred feet to the Leberion Plain.

When he found his first squad of eight, he addressed the team. "I have a recon mission for you at three o'clock. We've sighted an Invictus outpost near the location Mistress Regan will provide you. The area is hidden behind a shielding mist, but the Ruby Fae," here he inclined his head to Regan, "will perform a spell removal function as she did for Swanicott. What we need to know is the size and dispersal of Margetta's army camped around the Ancient Fae's fortress. Can I rely on you for this task?"

He smiled when a shout went up. He loved the heart of the warrior, always game.

"Regan will send the coordinates to Angus's cell." Angus led the squad. "It's also critical that you don't tell anyone what I've asked of you, including Mastyr Ben or the communication center or even Mastyr Stone. I have reasons for this."

Angus frowned. "Will there be others doing recon as well?"

Again, Ian hated lying, but he knew this mission had to proceed in secret. "A couple of others, but if you meet anyone along the way, I don't want any discussion between squads. Is that clear?"

"Yes, Mastyr." Angus spoke for the entire team.

"Just be sure to be at your assigned location at least fifteen minutes before three. The disguising mist should disperse at three sharp. Any questions?"

"Only one." Angus's eyes glowed with a familiar battle fervor. "When the mist disappears and we sight Invictus, do we engage?"

At that, a smile overspread Ian's lips. "At will."

Another shout went up.

Angus added. "We should do more of this, be on the offensive."

Ian clapped his shoulder. "I agree. But because I'm not sure of the numbers you'll be facing, if at any time it appears the squad will be overwhelmed, don't hesitate to retreat. Keep your heads. Think of this as a foray, not an overt battle. Understood?"

Each head bobbed.

"Good. And I want one of your team to remain behind to work with the local defense leaders of the communities assigned to your squad. Have these communities on the alert in case the Invictus show up." Ian met each warrior's gaze. "Again, be at your coordinates by two-forty-five and I'll be in touch with Angus before three."

Keeping Regan close, he headed to the next sector farther northeast along the foothill communities and received a similar, enthusiastic response. All the Guardsmen were ready to take charge and end the Invictus misery for good. With luck, tonight's effort would take them a good piece down the road.

Regan used her cell to establish the next set of coordinates and to keep a record of which team of Guardsmen would go where. Ian knew the names of all his men, so she made lists. She did this while he flew between sectors, at ease in his arms as though they'd flown together for decades instead of two nights.

Once all the squads took up a position near the fortress, each team would only be fifteen yards from the next. The warriors would no doubt start getting a picture that something big was going on. When the hour advanced to three, he'd begin pathing with the leaders to let them in on what he hoped to achieve. Once the squads were in position, his combined Vampire Guard and Shifter Brigade would surround Margetta's camp.

Ian knew his force wasn't near big enough to defeat such a large army. But by the time the battle ended with a strong retreat, he felt certain the Camberlaune warriors would have made a dent in the number of wraith-pairs ready to make war.

It would be one helluva a beginning.

~ ~ ~

Regan knew from various newspaper articles and blogs about Ian over the years that one of his favorite eateries was the Hungry

Troll in the central city of Hocklin. At midnight, he flew her there having made a reservation. The restaurant served specialty beers, several of them imported from the States through the Harrisburg Access Point.

When he touched down on the cobbled street, and she stepped off his booted foot, she became aware he was instantly the center of attention. He received many well-wishes from passing vehicles and a number of friendly back-slaps from pedestrians in the area.

Regan loved the good-naturedness of Realm-folk generally. And it pleased her that a man who sacrificed his personal contentment for his people, was appreciated so very much.

When a troll hurried to open the door for them both, she wasn't prepared for the sudden standing ovation and applause erupting from every single table of the pub-like establishment.

She looked up at Ian, wondering how he would take the adulation and she could see by his smile it pleased him. He lifted a hand, then graciously gestured to Regan.

If she'd been surprised before, she was astounded that she, too, received an incredibly warm welcome. When she glanced at Ian with a questioning brow, he pathed, *Everyone knows the part you played in the Swanicott victory. You're as beloved here as you are in your own realm.*

Tears started to her eyes. Sure, she'd helped out by getting rid of the disguising mist so that the Swanicott army could see the enemy, then engage. But she hadn't actually participated in the battle so she wasn't sure just how much adulation she deserved. But it meant a lot to her that her service had been appreciated.

She also lifted a hand and waved, then felt her cheeks grow warm as the applause continued. She wasn't used to so much attention.

A troll approached them. He wore a white apron, black vest and white shirt, had two menus in hand and a large belly. The latter was his best advertisement for the quality of the food.

He held his head high, beaming as he led them to a private booth at the back. To her surprise, she saw Ben standing against the wall near the bathrooms, scrolling through his cell.

For a moment, though, she got a very strange fae-ish feeling about Ben, as though something wasn't right. She focused on him, but the odd questioning response dissipated swiftly.

She gave her head a shake. The nature of the secret attack, as well as all she'd been through, seemed to be having an effect on her and not in a good way.

Ben's here, she pathed to Ian. She slid into the booth, the high maroon leather backs creating privacy for them.

I see him. I wonder what's going on.

Ben lifted his gaze from his phone and smiled. As Regan drew her menu into her hand, Ian waved for Ben to join them.

When Ben drew close, Ian asked. "Everything okay?"

Ben held up his cell. "Yes, very light activity tonight." He turned toward Regan. "How are you, Mistress? I think it's been thirty years since we last spoke."

"At least." Regan had to admit she'd never been completely at ease around the vampire, though she had no idea why.

During the time she'd dated Ian, Ben and his brother had been two of Ian's closest friends. Ben's brother, a mastyr as well, had died at Raven's Overlook during the massacre.

Maybe that was the reason she felt slightly ill-at-ease. Ben had suffered as both she and Ian had. And from what Ian had told her, Ben had taken his brother's death very hard.

Ben had long, curly blond hair, pulled back in the Guardsman's woven clasp. He had a regal bearing, a straight nose and straight brows. He was six-five and well-muscled though not as heavily as Ian. He wore a woven maroon shirt and the Guard outfit that had all eyes in the restaurant turned toward the two, handsome men.

Ben's smile was warm as he said, "I'll leave you both to your meals. The shepherd's pie is outstanding."

Ian asked him to join them, but he refused. He'd only wanted to touch base in person and to say hello to Regan since he hadn't had the chance the night before.

As he left, he stopped and chatted with a number of patrons along the way. He had an easy style, a perfect complement to Ian. Regan understood why the two men had been friends for such a long time.

During the meal, Ian grew very quiet as he ate his shepherd's pie. He'd ordered a local stout, but she wasn't sure he tasted much of either.

"What's bothering you?" she asked.

He lifted his gaze to her. "Is it that obvious?"

"Your head's down and you seem to be pathing with your food."

At that he smiled. "I want this to go well tonight." He kept his voice low.

"It will. You've done the right thing by keeping it on the down-low."

His mouth worked and after setting his fork on his plate, he twisted his thumb ring a few times. "I think I need to bring Stone in on this."

She nodded and using her fork, cut into a chicken filet covered with capers and lemon-butter sauce. "You want to add to the numbers." By this point she was whispering, afraid to reveal the secret plan to anyone who might be listening in on their conversation.

He switched to telepathy. *That's it exactly. My troops will be too spread out around the perimeter. And once the battling starts, it's hard for a warrior to retreat even when he's outnumbered. It goes against every instinct.*

She popped the bite into her mouth, following up with a sip of sweet German white wine. *What do your instincts tell you?*

At that, he chuckled.

"What? Why are you laughing?"

"I forgot how much your faeness slants your advice."

"Is that a bad thing?"

"No, it wasn't a criticism, I promise you. I'm surrounded by war-making vampires and shifters. We think in terms of weaponry, time and distance, numbers. Your advice leans toward intuition."

"We divine our answers as much by the subtle vibrations all around us. Like when I first saw Ben, what I noticed as he leaned against the wall checking his texts or email, was the glitter in his eye as though he was getting ready to do battle. I know he wasn't, but something about his expression didn't quite jive with being in a restaurant just to say hi to me."

Ian took a drink of the stout. "In this case, you're thinking like a fae. You forget, Ben makes war first, above everything else, just as I do. He could have easily been directing one of the squads to move to support another because of an Invictus attack."

"That makes total sense." She then switched the subject and asked about the quality of the stout and if he liked his meal.

He relaxed after that. She'd made the right decision not to press him about Ben.

Once she'd finished her dinner and Ian had as well, he led her outside. Again, he received the thanks of those passing by. When most of the well-wishing had subsided, he pulled out his cell and spoke in a quiet voice to Stone.

Regan also had two young fae women take her aside and ask about her retreat in Swanicott. Regan suggested they check out her website, which had all the information they would need to apply for entrance into one of a variety of programs her team offered.

Ian, a few feet away, replaced his cell in his pocket. He met her gaze and nodded, smiling. He looked pleased with Stone's response.

She was about to rejoin Ian, when a female shifter ran up to him and threw her arms around his neck. "Ian," she cried. "I haven't seen you in ages, not since you took me to your cave."

Ah, the infamous cave where he was supposed to have held two woman captive.

Ian smiled as he took hold of her arms and untangled the powerful looking woman from around his neck. Ah, a shifter female. "Janice. Don't you look pretty."

The shifter, at least six-two in height, had her blond hair teased to a massive height, sported long fake eyelashes and dark red lipstick. She wore a fringed black leather vest, cut low enough to reveal about five inches of cleavage, a really short, red skirt and black, thigh boots.

She didn't back up either, but planted her hand on Ian's arm and began to massage, stroking his bicep up and down. The movement was so suggestive, even the young fae women near Regan clucked their tongues in disapproval.

But Regan's reaction had her blood tattoos fired up and her heart beating faster and faster.

"So how's it hangin'?" Janice leaned in close. When she reached low, Regan could tell by the movement of the woman's arm, she'd just slid her hand between Ian's legs.

Regan had never felt such a quick, possessive response in her life. Nor had she ever moved as fast as she did now, pushing herself between Ian and his adoring fan.

"What the hell?" The shifter wasn't about to give up her ground, and immediately grabbed Regan by the shoulders ready to do battle.

But the blood tattoos had come to life and flowed with power.

In a swift move, Regan slid her hand up and placed it on Janice's forehead. She let an infinitesimal amount of her battle energy release. The shifter suddenly looked dazed as she stepped back, then slumped to her knees. She didn't pass out, but almost.

Ian shifted to stand beside Regan, his brows raised. "Did you just do what I think you did?"

"Yes. The same thing I did to the Invictus wraith in your home, except that I only used about a tenth of the power."

Janice recovered quickly, however, and gained her feet. She scowled at Regan, then peered at her. "You have a glowing red aura right now. Oh, sweet Goddess, you're the Ruby Fae."

Janice, bold as most shifters were, took Regan's right hand. "You sent power into my mind."

"I hope I didn't hurt you."

Janice shook her head, causing her long silver earrings to jangle. "No, not at all. It felt like a soft rain inside my head." She glanced at Ian then back to Regan. "And I'm so sorry. I didn't mean anything. I didn't know. You're with the mastyr, aren't you?"

Regan didn't want any confusion. "I am," she responded firmly.

"I apologize." She offered a sheepish smile. "I'm just so used to having free rein with Mastyr Ian." Her gaze lingered on him for a moment after which she turned to Regan and spoke in a low voice. "Has he taken you to his cave yet? If he hasn't, make him. It's beautiful. I think it would suit you." She then wished them both well and rejoined her friends waiting for her at the entrance to the restaurant.

She watched Janice go, but suddenly grew aware of how Ian's forest-fern scent now filled the air. She turned toward him. "Ian? What's going on?"

Chapter Eight

Everything with Regan was different this time around, including her aggression. He'd never seen her attack another Realm-person, especially not a powerful a shifter like Janice.

Where had this new boldness come from? Was it their shared tattoos, or because Regan had the blood rose phenomenon working in her?

Whatever it was, her intrusion into Janice's attentions had done more to fire up his blood than anything else could have.

He leaned close and sniffed her throat above her vein. *I can smell your blood. You've built a new supply for me, haven't you?*

Yes. Her voice, even inside his mind, sounded breathy. She'd begun to shed her mating scent as well, rich with jasmine and lime.

"Ian," she said quietly. "You should take me into the air. I think we have an audience."

He glanced around and saw she was right. At least three different knots of pedestrians were watching them.

He acted in one swift movement, dragging her against him and rising swiftly at the same time. He heard the small group of nearby Realm-folk issue a unison, 'Oh-h-h,' as he disappeared into the night sky.

Ian, did you settle things with Stone? Because I'm feeling the need for some alone time. I mean, really alone.

Stone is already getting things set up, bringing in his troops from Tannisford. I sent him the coordinates you prepared. He's following my protocol and keeping everything quiet. So, the answer is yes.

Because he held her tight against him, she had hold of each of his bare arms and dug in her nails. He groaned.

Can we go to the cave? The one Janice talked about?

Right now, I have something else in mind, something I think you'll love.

She slid an arm around his neck, pressing her body against him as he flew. He felt her lips on his cheek, his jaw, then lower as she half suckled, half kissed his throat. *I'd love to go lower, Ian. Really low.*

He grunted, the only sound he could make. He was hard as a rock and his brain kept rolling the images of Regan taking on Janice, then subduing the shifter female with a hand placed on her head.

Regan had staked a claim and he needed to respond in a way she would love and in a place he was sure she'd appreciate.

When he saw the gold gleam of the Camberlaune Fae Guild tower, he began his descent. He didn't aim for the building however, but deep into the grounds on the far side of the lake.

Your Guild, she pathed. *I haven't been here in ages.* He heard her quick intake of breath. *What a beautiful garden. And I remember now, the land was a gift.*

That's right. One of the wealthy fae leaders donated what was her family's quarry and surrounding property, as well as the money to fund the garden.

Very generous.

He scanned the area for Realm-folk of any kind, including Invictus, but all that returned was a cool December breeze. He dropped down beside a weeping willow.

A few months ago, he'd seen the tree from across the lake and knew it had possibilities for a hidden hook-up. He'd never imagined, however, that one night he'd be bringing Regan here.

He parted several drooping branches, revealing a private grassy space. He moved inside, taking her with him.

She turned in a circle. "You're right. I love it."

"I thought you would." He kissed her. She cooed in response, her arms snaking around his neck once more and holding him tight.

Her scent was heavy in the air, letting him know he was on the right track.

Ian, this is perfect. Exactly what I need. Watching Janice fondle you got my blood all worked up. I can't explain it, but my desire for you exploded.

Mine, too.

He lifted her off her feet, carrying her to the tree trunk, settling her against it. "Are you comfortable? Because I'm thinking this should be hard and fast." He released her enough so that her feet once more touched the ground.

She shivered then wiggled her back against the tree. "This will work." She glanced from one side to the other, whispering, "Is anyone out there? I mean, is there a chance we'll be seen or overheard?"

"I saw very few in the garden and none as far out as this tree. We're good." He dropped to unzip her ankle boots, then took off her jeans. He was pretty sure her thong got lost somewhere down one of her jean leg-holes.

He let his Guard coat fall to the grass then unzipped. He didn't bother with his boots, not for what he meant to do. He leaned in and kissed her again, plunging his tongue in and out.

She crossed her arms over the back of his neck, holding him tight as soft moans sounded in her throat.

With his hips connected to hers, he rubbed his cock down her cleft. Her hips arched into him, begging for more.

He then lifted one of her legs to his waist, afterward raising the other and getting her settled in.

He drew back so he could look at her. Her dark eyes glittered with desire and her lips were swollen. "Ian." She arched her hips.

"What do you want, Regan? You have to tell me."

A soft smile curved her lips. "Your cock, plunging deep."

He'd always loved how direct she was with him.

When she locked her legs around his waist, he dipped his hand between their bodies and guided his cock to her well. The sweet scent of her sex wafted up as he continued to kiss her.

He thrust in a long slow glide. She was so wet, so ready for him. He groaned. *You feel amazing, Regan.*

And I could worship you on my knees, Ian.

His body jerked in response at the image her words conjured, of her mouth surrounding his cock, of her tongue licking, hands fondling.

Tell me what you'd do, Regan, only whisper it out loud.

He drew back, thrusting steadily now.

"I'd be on my knees without anything on. I'd tease your cock until it stood straight out, then swipe the tip with my tongue over and over. But you'd have to beg me to do more. Would you beg me, Ian?"

"Hell, yeah." He nodded, moving his hips faster. "And after I begged?"

"I'd get down to business. I'd take you in my mouth and suck for as long as you wanted me to."

He moved faster now. "What else would you do?"

"Ian," she cried. "Oh, God."

Seeing she was almost ready to come, he slowed the tempo, easing her back a little. "I want to hear it all, Regan. I want to feel like I'm coming in your mouth as I release. Will you do that for me? Talk to me while I come?"

She gripped his arms, stroking him, her hips matching his in hard, responsive pulses to each of his thrusts. "I'd take as much of you in my mouth as I could, and I'd beg you to mouth-fuck me. Would you do that, Ian? Would you fuck my mouth with your dick?"

"Yes." His voice was low and hoarse, his balls getting tight. He drove into her faster still.

She was breathing hard as she continued, "With each thrust, I'd suck, then drag my lips in a tight circle as you pulled back. I'd keep sucking and dragging, catching the head each time. You'd go faster and faster, like you are now, only in my mouth."

"I'm so hard for you. Are you close?"

"Right on the edge."

"Then let's do this." He went faster, his cock pistoning.

"And one more thing, Ian. I'd take your come in my mouth, all of it."

He gave a shout and his seed flew like lightning through his cock. When she started to scream, he covered her mouth with his hand. Her body jerked and writhed beneath his as he plundered her sex.

He kept driving into her until the last bit of pleasure pulsed through him. Still connected, he smiled at the satisfied look in her eye, even though she breathed in gasps against his hand. He was taking in deep gulps himself.

When he could trust her, he uncovered her mouth and chuckled softly. "Hope I didn't distress you with my hand, but I didn't want anyone to think a woman was being murdered in here."

She laughed in response then rested her arms on his shoulders. With a smile, she leaned up to kiss him. "It was perfect, beginning to end." However, her brows rose. "There's only one problem." She glanced down at where they were still connected. "You leave a lot behind, you know. And I didn't exactly come prepared."

He reached into his back pocket and took out a kerchief. "Thought we might need this." Pulling out of her, he tucked the square of linen between her legs, holding it in place as she lowered her legs.

"Thank goodness you had this kind of foresight."

He chuckled again. "Let's put it this way, I've been in a constant aroused state since I caught your blood rose scent. I figured this would happen sooner or later."

~ ~ ~

Regan didn't know what to make of their current situation. He'd been right to plan ahead and he'd been really right about their mutual lust for each other. She couldn't have refused him even if she'd wanted to.

Which she didn't.

She'd been without a man for a long time now and wherever this led, she appreciated the sex. There, she'd admitted it to herself. She'd missed romping in bed with him, or on ottomans, or beneath weeping willows. She wondered if Ian had ever thought about doing it in the air.

"You're smiling. No, I'd call that a grin. What are you thinking?"

"You don't want to know."

"Tell me. Now."

Having found her thong halfway down the right leg of her pants, she put it on then pulled up her jeans and zipped. "Have you ever had sex while levitating or even flying?"

He threw his head back and laughed. "Honey, I'm game if you are. But no, I've never done that before."

"We might have to give it a shot." She pulled her sweater down, then dropped to the grass and slid on her ankle boots, zipping up each in turn.

"I'll say this again. For such a spiritual being, you're very physical."

"The two aren't mutually exclusive."

He nodded, smiling once more.

When she stood up, she saw he'd turned his back to her and was using a couple of fingers to part the draped willow branches.

"Looking for Invictus sign?"

"Always. The skies look clear, though. No sign of a red wind. And I've been thinking. We should head to Grasmer then Clarefield to make an appearance. I'll contact Ben and Stone again to let them know where we'll be."

"Sounds like a plan."

He turned toward her, looking her up and down. "The kerchief?"

She felt a blush climb her cheeks. "Um, I'm keeping it with me for the time being."

"Shit. I'm not thinking. Let me fly you to my home near Gasmer. We can both clean up."

"Now that does sound like a plan."

He flew her swiftly in the direction of the north-central plain city. From what she knew, Gasmer now had a population of fifty-thousand Realm-folk, though she remembered it as a village of only a couple hundred.

Just as he passed over a well-lit street, however, he veered sharply left.

She didn't know why until she saw the cause; two shifters had fought and killed an Invictus pair right beneath a streetlight. Several Realm-folk stood back, watching.

When he touched down, Regan had to hold her nose. The smell was awful.

"Mastyr Ian." The taller of the two shifters with blood spatter across his face, chest and arms, nodded to Ian, then to Regan. "Apologies for the mess." He swiped his cheek with his sleeve.

Ian kept his arm around her waist. "Just checking to see if you needed help."

The shifter offered a wry grin. "Nope. But these two have been around a long time and were hard to take down."

"Really hard," the other shifter said, a deep frown between his brows. "But we got 'em."

"Then there was no way to save them for rehab."

"Sorry, Mastyr, but no. We would have needed a few more shifters for that."

Ian waved a hand. "We all do what we can."

The taller of the two scratched his forehead. Something was on his mind. Lowering his voice, he said, "We're looking forward to the recon foray later. But … "

"What is it? Don't hold back."

"Mastyr Ben was here earlier, asking questions. Didn't feel right to lie to him."

"Sorry to put you in that position, but I need you to keep your mission a complete secret. I'll explain everything to Ben later. He'll understand."

Regan had long since looked away from the Invictus pair on the ground and was grateful when Ian took to the skies once more. She drew a deep breath. "The smell surprised me."

"Gut wounds are the worst. The intestines open up."

She forced her stomach to settle down, swallowing hard a few times.

"I need to contact Ben, see if he's getting suspicious." Regan sensed when Ian began pathing with his second-in-command.

She turned her attention to the lights in the town below. So much had changed in Camberlaune over the centuries, she hardly recognized any of the places she'd seen so far.

She felt Ian grow tense as he began his descent. She knew he'd disconnected his telepathic conversation with Ben. "Everything okay?"

"Just feeling guilty. I really hate keeping Ben in the dark. He asked if I'd been setting up some kind of mission into the mountains, so I told him a half-truth that I was sending three or four teams on recon work. He said I should have told him."

"What did you say to that?"

Ian crossed a small range of rolling hills, then descended into the backyard of a modern dwelling. "I lied. I said I thought I had."

"Did he believe you?"

"Nope, but he let it go."

Regan looked around. "This is a lovely home. By the way, exactly how many places do you have?"

"Five. Six including the lake cave."

"I really have to see that cave."

"At some point, I'm sure you will." He was smiling as he set her down on the lawn.

When she hopped off his boot, he led her into the house by way of the backdoor. She glanced up and saw the steel shutters ready to come down near dawn against so much glass.

The house was single story and he walked her to the master bedroom. Once there, he gestured to the bathroom. "The hamper's right outside the door."

"Perfect." She'd had plenty of sex over the years, but sometimes the logistics afterward could be crazily embarrassing.

After cleaning up, she put the kerchief in the hamper. Ian stood near the foot of the bed, waiting for her. He'd donned a black tank, fresh leathers and even wore a different pair of thigh boots that had skulls running down the outside seams.

She couldn't help but smile. "Zane would love those."

Ian laughed. "They were a gift from him. I don't wear them often, but given what we're be heading into, I liked the idea."

She glanced at his rings. "When did you start wearing so much hardware? You never used to."

"About the same time I got the tattoo." He patted his chest. "A couple decades ago, I'd been in a close up battle with three Invictus pair and one of the vampires wore rings. Damn, they hurt when he fought. Afterward, I was bruised like I'd never been before. I made the decision then and there to add them to my uniform."

She looked him up and down. "It's pretty intimidating." And other things she didn't need to mention or she'd end up in his arms again.

Checking her internal clock, she could tell it was almost two-thirty. Her heartrate jumped. "We should probably head to the Dauphaires."

"Yep. You still feel confident about the de-spelling process?"

She drew in a ragged breath, more from excitement than anything else. "I do, but I'll need to be in a meditative state. Will you have Guardsmen nearby for protection? Because I'm thinking you'll need to be guarded if you're supporting me."

"Already thought of that. I'll have a dozen of my most powerful warriors standing watch."

"Then we're ready."

"We are."

Now that the time had come, Regan felt tense and jumpy as though electricity flowed through her veins, but in a really good way. Angus was right; taking charge rocked.

~ ~ ~

Ian flew Regan directly to the granite outcrop that overlooked Dark Gorge. The mist closest to them had the same disrupted appearance from Regan's earlier efforts. The rest looked intact, but he couldn't help but wonder if Margetta had inadvertently discovered this disturbed part of her spell.

Whatever the case, the die was cast and there was nothing more to do than to let the plan unfold.

Just past 2:30, with his plans in place, he saw no reason not to involve Ben. He pathed him then gave a quick rundown on what was happening.

He expected Ben to be pissed at him for not including him, but Ben responded, *I totally get your need for secrecy. I'd suspected for a long time someone was leaking information to the Ancient Fae, but I had the worst time thinking it was any of our Guardsmen.*

Same here. He and Ben had always had similar attitudes and views, one reason he trusted Ben as he did. *Why don't you head out here? We're about to engage the enemy.*

You know there's nowhere else I want to be.

Ian gave him his position. Ben was a quick flyer and it wouldn't take him but a few minutes to join Ian.

And the offensive starts at three?

Yes.

Is Regan with you right now?

For the moment. But once she's destroyed Margetta's spell, I'm planning to move her to the south side of Dark Gorge. I'll have a couple of our warriors guarding her.

Sounds like you have everything in hand. And Ian, this is exactly what we've needed to do for a long time. I'll see you in a few.

Reverting his attention to Regan, he pathed, *Everything's set with Ben. He's on his way.*

Was he upset you hadn't involved him initially?

Not really. I think he trusts my judgment. He held her gaze. *Are you ready for this?*

Absolutely.

He could feel her energy rising and he could relate. Whatever this was for Regan, he was going into battle and his warrior nerves were hopping, ready to go.

Caris Roane

He moved in behind her as he had earlier when she'd first experimented with breaking down the initial layer of mist. He sensed her drop into her meditative process as she relaxed against him.

I want you to wait before you sink too far, he pathed. *I want the Guardsmen in place who I've assigned to protect both you and me while you're working on the counter-spell.*

I've thought of that, too. I'm resting just inside the deeper state. I won't sink 'til you tell me.

He loved that she was in step with him. *Good. Are your eyes closed?*

Yes.

He watched as another squad arrived. He inclined his head to them as they continued on to their designated coordinates.

To Regan, he pathed, *Several of the teams have passed by, those heading to the westernmost reaches. We're on our way.*

He felt her breathe a sigh of relief. *Sounds like everything's moving as planned.*

A moment later, the first of the squads he'd assigned to serve as their detail, arrived at the granite outcrop. Each warrior landed lightly and though nodding to Ian, stayed in silent mode. He took a moment to path to the leader, letting him know what was really going on. The squad leader then pathed to his team. Excitement vibrated in the air.

Once they were all in position, he used hand signals to direct them to form an arc in front of the two of them, with three protecting the rear. As battle frequencies rose, the men fanned out. His own powerful energy radiated down his arms, preparing to erect his shield when necessary. As a result, his blood tattoos heated up.

Ian continued contacting the various squad leaders telepathically. He let them know what was really happening, that his force and part of Stone's were heading into battle with Margetta's primary army. What returned each time was a telepathic cheer, for he could call it nothing less.

Shifters began to arrive as well. The squad leaders pathed to him, letting him know their teams were taking up the easternmost positions as ordered. Again, Ian let them in on the true nature of the mission. Even if one of them was a spy and informed Margetta, she wouldn't have enough time to remove her army. She could move a small portion of it, but not the majority.

When Stone checked in and the last unit was in place, he pathed to Regan, *Game time. Let your magic rip.*

~ ~ ~

Regan readied herself to drop into her deepest meditative state in order to create her counter-spell once more. Before she began, however, she pathed to Ian, *Place your hands on my blood tattoos the way you did last time and let your power flow. I can't tell you how much your battle energy supports my spell-making.*

Whatever you need, Regan. Let me know, and I'll do it.

When he slid his hands to connect fully with her blood tattoos, his battle vibration hummed against her skin. She deepened her meditation until she reached a perfect place of connection with all things realm.

She opened her inner eye to see Margetta's spell and to once again appreciate its complexity and beauty.

She began, as she had earlier in the night, to compose the counter-spell, a process using many of the elements in Margetta's spell base. The moment it came together, her blood tattoos lit on fire.

Ian pathed. *You're ready, aren't you?*

I am. Do I need to hold back?

Nope. Your timing's perfect.

Then start letting your battle energy flow like last time. As the first layer begins to dissipate, I'll begin composing the second counter-spell. There are five in all, but this will happen very fast, Ian, in waves only a few seconds apart. Ready?

Hell, yeah. Just give me one sec.

She felt him switch his telepathy from just her to his squad leaders. Because he included her in what proved to be a group contact, she heard the orders he delivered to his Guardsmen and shifter warriors. The vampire had power.

What returned felt like a big cheer, definitely a flow of excitement and energy that almost pulled her out of her conjuring state.

Let it loose, Ian pathed, though just to her this time.

Regan brought the initial counter-spell to the forefront of her mind. Using the enormous shared power emanating from the blood-tattoos, she let the spell flow.

It was like fire from her arms and hands. Part of her wanted to watch the mist disperse, but she had to stay focused on creating and launching the successive counter-spells.

Ian pathed, *The first layer is gone.*

She quickly brought the second combination of melodies, words and images together. *I'm releasing the second wave.*

I feel it. The layer is peeling away. I'm watching the whole thing and it's amazing.

She fashioned the third and with Ian's battle energy flowing, she launched it.

Then the fourth.

Finally, the fifth.

Holy shit. It's gone. All of it. Sweet Goddess. But you'd better come back to me as in now. Something's not right.

Regan returned to full consciousness, but didn't immediately move her arms or disengage from Ian's power. Together, they were still streaming the spells and it would take some time to roll back the disguising mist from all over the large acreage of Margetta's land.

But what stunned her was how close the fortress actually was. The mist had not only disguised its existence but also its proximity to the gorge. It wasn't more than a quarter mile distant.

Yet the tents in front of them seemed too quiet. Where were the Invictus?

Ian, what's going on?

I'm not sure. Where's the army?

Regan's heartrate doubled. *I can feel they're here. I can sense them. Oh, no.*

What?

Ian, you'd better contact everyone. There's another layer to the spell and I'll need a minute.

As Ian delivered the warning, Regan dove deep again and once more summoned Margetta's spell.

Sure enough, a sixth layer emerged, this one more intricate than the others.

Fear beat at her, that she and Ian would be slaughtered in what was an extremely vulnerable position. Despite that her knees shook, she forced herself to focus on the sixth spell. No wonder the fortress had been invisible for so long.

Fortunately, the same essential base appeared and after sorting through it and separating the various incantations, melodic choices and special words, she found the final layer. She quickly created the counter-spell and let it fly. Ian's power flared, and as she opened her eyes, dozens of Invictus pairs suddenly became fully visible.

Ian had already ordered his nearby force to hold the line until he could take care of business. But he now pathed the team leaders with a different directive. *Engage at will,* resounded through her mind and therefore to the rest of the squads. Aloud, he again reminded his closest warriors to wait for his command.

Shifting to face her, he gripped her shoulders. "You've done your part, and I need to fight. Two of my men will take you to the opposite side of the gorge to protect you. Stay hidden in the forest until I come for you."

He gestured to the Guardsmen behind them. "Sean, you'll see to this?"

"Yes, Mastyr." Sean had thick, red hair and a determined look as he nodded to her. "Can you fly, Mistress?"

"Yes, absolutely."

Levitating, he waved a hand toward Dark Gorge. "Then, let's get you out of here."

Regan immediately took to the air, moving as fast as she could to the opposite side. Landing at the edge of the forest, she slipped among the trees. The Guardsmen came with her.

Each stood facing away from her and far enough apart that she could see the granite outcropping. Ian had set up a powerful blue shield behind which his troops battled the Invictus.

But there were so many.

Regan had hoped Ian's forces would be able to take the fortress, even though she knew the odds were against them. But with so many pairs battling, she didn't see how it would be possible.

Chapter Nine

With the enemy encampment now fully exposed, and Regan safely away from the north side of the gorge, Ian focused all his attention on the coming battle. His men had already formed a line in front of the Invictus force, each having erected a battle shield. He then let loose his own battle energy and added to the heavy shield wall.

Many of the wraiths rose into the air, shrieking. Their bonded mates formed an opposing line to Ian's Vampire Guard, then shouted, roared and struck their weapons together to create as much noise as possible.

They were fierce-looking with wild hair, and a battle fervor equal to his Guardsmen. They wore lots of leather, heavy boots, chains and spikes.

Ian wasn't fooled by their crude appearance, however. Their increased power because of the Invictus bond made them dangerous.

Red battle shields accompanied the Invictus, a counterpart to the Guardsmen's shields that now vibrated in a blue wave of energy in front of him.

"Hold steady," he shouted.

His troops obeyed.

He wanted the Invictus to break ranks first. By nature, the bond also created chaos and wraith-pairs were easier to defeat one-on-one.

Ian's blood tattoos were lit up and even at a distance he felt Regan's power flowing toward him, focused on him. What would it be like if he bonded with her?

Ian tracked a powerful wraith who never took her gaze off him. She moved steadily closer to his position, though remaining high in the air. No doubt she was planning to dive-bomb.

When the wraith was directly above him, she flipped in the air, head down, her palms lighting up a dark red. At the same time, the Invictus charged forward.

The moment had come.

"Attack at will," he shouted.

Almost as one, his Guardsmen launched.

He released his shield, more than ready to engage *mano-a-mano*. He arched his neck, lifted his glowing palms as the woman fired then let his battle energy fly. The resulting clash of frequencies sent explosions of blue and red sparks into the air.

This one had power.

When her gaze flipped for a split-second to his right, by long habit, Ian levitated backward in a quick dart of movement. Her shifter mate's axe struck the granite where Ian had been standing, the sound reverberating down the gorge.

The pair moved toward him with one mind. The wraith opened her mouth, exposing sharp, yellow fangs then let loose with an ear-shattering shriek. But he was used to the sound so he ignored her, focusing instead on building up the power in his hands.

His battle energy flowed once more down both arms, his blood tattoos pulsing. The wraith, streaking back and forth through the air, was firing hers up again, which meant he could expect her bonded shifter to come at him.

The shifter's eyes were bloodshot, his skin ruddy, and his long, black hair hung in filthy strands to his waist. His nostrils worked like bellows as he sprouted wolf fur down his bare chest.

Ian felt a surge of power from his blood tattoos. He shot forward faster than he ever had before, swiped the axe from the shifter's hands and used the blunt end to smash into the back of his head.

The man went sprawling, landing face down on the granite and sliding almost to the edge of the gorge cliff.

His mate shrieked, faltering in the air, then landing hard on her side. She shook her head and rose unsteadily to her feet. A series of dull shrieks followed as she went to her mate and flopped down beside him.

They shared their power and when either was badly wounded, the other couldn't keep going.

He moved off to the side to keep an eye on the pair he'd just wounded as well as the battle.

But as he analyzed the battlefield, at first, he didn't understand what he was looking at since there was so little movement. The Guard that had served to protect himself and Regan, stood over several either dead or incapacitated wraith-pairs.

Otherwise, the field looked empty though there had to be a hundred tents directly in front of them, leading up to the fortress.

A few more of his Guardsmen had come in from their positions both east and west of his and were now moving from tent to tent as well.

When his squad leaders started checking in with the same disturbing reports, of encountering only a handful of easily dispatched wraith-pairs, Ian's heart sank.

Where the hell was Margetta's army? Was it possible she'd actually been able to move thousands of her troops within the last few minutes?

Instinctively, Ian knew the Ancient Fae didn't have that kind of power. She would have required at least twenty, maybe thirty minutes to relocate an army of this size. Yet, once the spell dissipated, she would have only had a couple of minutes to get the job done and that was impossible.

Which meant only one thing.

Somehow, though he'd been careful, the Ancient Fae had learned of his plans in sufficient time to save the bulk of her forces. But who had told her? Who was Camberlaune's traitor?

~ ~ ~

Regan heard Ben call out her name and she responded until she could tell he was moving through the forest in her direction. Yet the moment she saw him, she knew something was off. For one thing, she felt his battle energy revving up.

The Guardsmen greeted him and he smiled, then lifted glowing blue palms in their direction.

Regan didn't have time to do more than utter a startled cry as he fired at both vampires, hitting each in the chest. They flew backward, one landing against a tree and the other falling into a dense thicket of shrubs.

She stared at the men, horror-stricken. Their chests were caved in, smoke curled from their bodies and the stench had her stomach boiling. The men were dead.

"Let's go, Regan. And in case you're wondering, you'll be bonding with me. I'm the one Margetta has chosen for you."

Regan had to get out of there, fast. She levitated to make her escape, but Ben was a blur as he grabbed her. He then planted his hand on her head and her mind grew strangely fluid. Not a single thought could emerge except that she felt so tired and wanted to sleep.

Ben picked her up, cradling her in his arms. *That's it, Regan. A little trick Margetta taught me. Now, let yourself go.*

Just before she fell unconscious, she felt herself flying through the air.

~ ~ ~

By the time Ian heard back from his squad leaders, he had all the confirmation he needed that Margetta had received a warning of the impending attack. The camp still had fires burning, food cooking in skillets, water boiling in pots. She'd removed her army with the formidable power she had at her fingertips but she'd begun the process long before Regan had destroyed the spell.

Ian kept shaking his head. He'd been damn careful. How could she have known?

His forward Guardsmen continued to plow through tent after tent, heading toward the stone fortress. But the response was always the same. The Invictus were gone.

When he reached the wall of the fortress, the same place he'd caught Regan in his arms two nights earlier, he had a sick feeling something had happened that he couldn't face, couldn't believe.

At least Regan was safe on the far side of the gorge.

He reached for Stone, pathing, *What are you finding?*

Nothing. There's nothing here. Half my warriors encountered no Invictus at all. The rest battled a handful of wraith-pairs. That's it.

Ian shook his head. *Meet me at the fortress entrance. I think it's on the north side.*

I'll bring some of my men.

Ian ordered his Guardsmen to make a clean sweep of the adjacent forest all the way to the gorge to make certain the Invictus really were gone. He then pathed to his squad leaders, directing them and their troops to do the same, including those belonging to his Shifter Brigade.

He levitated slowly to have a look, doing a 360 spin at the same time. He visually hunted for any sign of the enemy, but he found nothing. He then flew higher into the air to get a birds-eye view of the encampment. What he saw stunned him. He did a cursory estimate and realized he was looking at over five thousand tents.

Margetta's army was beyond anything the ruling mastyrs had ever imagined. No wonder Regan had said that the woman didn't seem worried. But how had Margetta known to remove her army?

It appeared he'd been right after all, he had a spy in his Guard or maybe the Brigade. But his mind refused to speculate who this might be.

That sick, twisted feeling returned, something so heinous that bile crawled up his throat. Part of him knew he was witnessing a traitorous act of enormous magnitude, but another part couldn't even look it.

He saw the tower where Regan had been imprisoned. At least he knew she was safe from Margetta. He'd left two guards with her.

He made his descent on the north lawn where he could see Stone standing in a knot of his warriors.

Stone pulled away from the group. "Ian, what the fuck happened here? It's as though they knew we were coming and pulled out."

"I think that's exactly what happened." Ian's temples throbbed. "But I don't know how. I was so damn careful. Were you?" Maybe Stone was at fault.

"Shit, yes. I told no one, as requested. Not even my seconds."

"I didn't either." A sharp pain drilled through his head. "Except ... "

Stone took hold of his arm, gripping it hard. "Ian? Who did you tell?"

Ian couldn't breathe and the pain in his head felt like someone had suddenly jammed a hot poker inside his skull. In that moment, his world flipped upside down and everything he knew to be true no longer was.

As he stared hard at nothing in particular, Ian's perspective began to shift. Raven's Overlook slipped into his mind, the horror, the carnage, the loss of those he loved.

"I don't get it. *His* brother died there. His more *powerful* brother. Which would mean he'd planned his death."

Stone shook Ian's arm. "Whose brother? Talk to me."

He met Stone's gaze, but shook his head back and forth. "This can't be possible. I have to be wrong. Otherwise what happened here tonight began five-hundred years ago. It can't be true."

Stone yanked his arm hard. "Fuck it, talk to me. You know who it is, don't you?"

It could only be one person, but Ian couldn't speak the name aloud.

He jerked his arm away and thrust his hands into his hair, dislodging the woven clasp. He'd chosen to believe Ben. That was what came to him. Ben had said Regan had enthralled him. Those had been Ben's words all those centuries ago. And Ian had believed him.

Ravens Overlook.

All the dead.

His sister ripped to pieces, her babies with her.

He heard a loud wind, or sound, or something. But it was coming out of his throat.

He levitated then took off flying north. Maye he could escape the truth if he flew fast enough.

Stone ghosted his movements, tracking with him.

For the last several centuries, Ian had cast all the blame at Regan's feet. But the whole time, a snake had slithered through Camberlaune, feeding Ian's mind with poison.

But what else had Ben done on his watch? What other nightmares had he instigated?

Ian recalled the attack on Westbreak Village two-hundred years ago. Though it wasn't as severe as Raven's Overlook, some had called it a massacre because thirty Realm-folk had died, including two of his most powerful Guardsmen. One of them had been a mastyr equal to Ben.

Ian could recall a couple more incidences where powerful mastyrs had died in the midst of an Invictus blitz attack. He had to conclude these hadn't been random after all. Ben was just getting rid of his competition.

Holy fuck. Never had a vampire been so ambitious, so ruthless as Ben. And Ian hadn't seen it.

When the storm of awareness finally passed, Ian was left with an ice cold sensation throughout his body that made his fingers ache.

Slowly, he came back to himself and levitated midair to gain his bearings. He'd been moving steadily north and was somewhere over the Dauphaire Mountains.

The air was freezing cold, matching the frost in his veins.

Stone said nothing, just stuck close as Ian turned to head back the way he'd come, back to the fortress.

But something else nagged at him, something he'd forgotten.

What was the last thing Ben had said to him?

A new kind of dread filled him as he recalled everything he'd told Ben.

Come with me, he pathed to Stone.

I'm with you, brother.

Ian picked up speed, his blood tattoos throbbing hot now.

He'd covered over fifty miles from the time his mind had connected the dots.

When he reached the granite outcrop, he zeroed in on the opposite side of the gorge where he knew Regan and his two Guardsmen had flown.

He crossed, landing at the edge of the trees, then moved inside.

He could smell death before he reached the bodies.

Two good men lay with chests and internals fried, the skin blackened around the edges from a powerful battle blast.

"Damn all the elf lords to hell," Stone said. "What happened here?"

In a monotone, Ian told him everything he'd just figured out.

Stone listened. "But if Margetta could get to Ben … "

"She didn't. I'm convinced Ben went to her and offered himself up. In fact, I'm sure of it. He's been aligned with her since before Raven's Overlook."

"You believe he was responsible for the massacre."

"Yes. He needed to make sure his brother died."

Stone scowled. "I don't get it. Why would he do that?"

"His brother had more essential power. If something happened to me, Ben's brother would have ruled."

"The devil is in this."

Ian blinked, a slow painful dip of his lids. "He separated me from Regan. She was too powerful as well. She was a threat to his plans, especially being fae. She'd picked up on something earlier tonight at the midnight meal. Ben had been there and she'd said something was off. I paid no attention. It was a fae thing, which I can't relate to, so I discounted it. But this … "

He glanced around as though looking for something, but didn't know what.

"Ian." Stone's voice sounded a mile distant.

"What?"

"Where's Regan?"

The full reality hit Ian like a heavy blow to his chest. Once more he roared into the night air, rising swiftly and shouting his rage.

Ben had Regan and there was no doubt in his mind he had one intention, to force the blood rose bond.

Worse, he didn't even know where to begin the hunt.

~ ~ ~

Regan woke up with her arms on fire.

Pain.

So much pain.

"There you are." She recognized Margetta's voice, the lovely melodic sound that hid the woman's venom. "I guess this must hurt."

Regan opened her eyes and tried to lift her right arm. But she was bound to the side of the bed. Margetta had both her hands over the blood tattoos, working to remove them.

"Are you using your battle energy?" Regan could hardly breathe the pain was so bad.

"Yes. I tried a spell, but I couldn't easily break through this strange blood-bond you created with Mastyr Ian. So I'm frying your skin. It's working very well and will have the same effect as a counter-spell, but in a tenth of the time."

Regan sank into the pain, letting it roll over her. She drifted once more into unconsciousness.

She didn't know how much time had passed before a scent like eucalyptus brought her around. When she opened her eyes, she saw that Margetta held a sachet beneath her nose.

"Good. You're back."

The pain had diminished to a dull throb, something she could bear. At the same time, she sent healing into her arms. "Where am I?"

"What does it matter? You're mine now and very soon, you'll serve me."

She glanced around. "Not the fortress, I see."

"No. Unfortunately, your boyfriend overran it with his force and some of Stone's army as well. So, this will have to do. This is one of Ben's homes. But don't think you'll be rescued. No one knows about this dwelling and I've set up a spell to guard it."

Regan stared at the scourge of the Nine Realms. She recalled the beauty of the woman's spells. "What happened to you?"

Margetta leaned back slightly. "You mean, to make me the way I am?"

"Yes. Your spells are beautiful. Melodic and poetic."

Margetta laughed. "Your compliments will not save you."

"But I'd like to know."

Margetta shrugged. "You want to know if daddy tortured and raped me. Well, he didn't. I had a lovely upbringing. I just got bored of life, especially as my powers grew. One day, I decided that no matter how long it took, I would rule the Nine Realms." Her lips curved. "And I will."

She then snapped her fingers. "Come, Ben. We're almost ready here."

Regan shifted and saw Ben push away from a wood-paneled wall. So, she'd been right about him. "You killed two of your Guardsmen to get to me."

"Two of Ian's. They were never mine."

"They didn't know that. They served you as though you were the mastyr."

He lifted his chin, his eyes colder than she'd ever seen them. "But I wasn't, was I?"

Her mind rolled back to the massacre. "You planned and executed what happened at Raven's Overlook."

"Of course."

"Including feeding Ian's beliefs I was to blame, and that I'd enthralled him."

"Ian's guilt ruled him. It wasn't hard to make you the scapegoat and it was the best way to get rid of your influence. You were too powerful, even back then. I knew if you stayed with Ian, one day you'd see me for what I am. I couldn't take the risk. I thought about killing you outright, but that would have alerted Ian that something else was going on."

She sank back onto the pillows. Somehow she'd ended up abducted by Margetta twice in little over a month. Now she was strapped to a bed with Ben ready to make use of her blood rose powers by bonding with her.

How had this happened?

She dropped swiftly into her meditative state, then attempted to path Ian. *Are you there?*

"Not gonna happen." Margetta put her hand on Regan's head.

Pain sliced through her so fast that Regan cried out and sudden tears poured from her eyes. A blocking spell formed at the same time.

"You gonna do that again?"

Regan shook her head. "No, I guess not."

Though the agony had passed, Regan's head throbbed. She accessed her healing vibration and let it flow. In doing so, however, she could tell that the spell Margetta had installed would deliver pain whenever she attempted to path anyone.

How would Ian ever find her if she couldn't communicate with him? Besides, she still didn't even know where she was. Ben's home could be anywhere in Camberlaune.

Margetta released the bindings on Regan's arm. She could move now and pulled both arms over her chests protectively.

Ben drew close, settling his hand on her shoulder. She could hear him draw in a deep breath. "What am I smelling? A very rich fragrance, very floral." He released his breath, closing his eyes at the same time. "So this is what it's like. To be near a blood rose."

Regan had two thoughts at once. First was a realization the blood tattoos were completely gone and no longer protected her. Second, she thought Ben the most beautiful vampire she'd ever seen.

She could also tell he needed to feed.

As one in a trance, she sat up and extended her arm to him. "Take from my vein."

~ ~ ~

Ian flew back over the Dauphaire Mountains, hunting for Regan, crisscrossing the land faster than he ever had before. He kept calling out to her telepathically, but nothing returned to him. He'd left Stone in charge of combing the fortress and the deserted camp for anything that could help him locate Margetta or Regan.

But searching in this way made little sense. Ben had her, which meant she was back under Margetta's thumb. It wouldn't do much good to use a scattergun approach in trying to find her.

Reaching the northeastern section of the mountains, he headed to his cabin. A few minutes later, he landed on the deck and paced the length in quick hard strides, shoving his hair away from his face since the clasp was long gone.

A sickness had taken hold of him, a guilt so profound he could hardly breathe. He'd misjudged Regan for five long centuries. He'd convinced himself she'd enthralled him, that she alone was responsible for Raven's Overlook.

Instead – Goddess help him – the horrendous killing had been orchestrated by Ben. Ian couldn't fathom how he'd completely misjudged the man. How could a warrior he'd trusted with his life, for such a long time, have done these terrible things?

He continued to march. He had to think this through, had to figure out how to find Regan.

He paused in his marching and lifted his arms up. He'd been so caught up in his distress he hadn't realized the blood tattoos had now disappeared. Margetta had severed his connection to Regan, leaving her vulnerable to another mastyr, to Ben.

In sheer agony, he dropped to his knees and roared into the night sky. This was Margetta's work. He could feel it in his bones.

But how had he gotten here? Was it truly because he'd trusted the wrong person all these years?

A cool night breeze blew along the deck, lifting his hair.

In the end, this was all his fault.

When he thought back to the massacre, especially to the horror of finding his beautiful sister dead, he'd fallen into his grief then and there. He remembered feeling like he'd been thrown into a pit he'd never be able to escape.

Regan had been with him. She'd sought comfort in his arms, but he'd pushed her away. Somehow, she was responsible for the massacre, at least that's what he'd chosen to believe. Whether she'd enthralled him or not, his love, desire and need for her had kept him from Camberlaune.

For a long time afterward, Ben had remained silent. But at what moment had he started to support Ian's conviction Regan had been to blame for Raven's Overlook? Was it Ben who had first suggested Regan had enthralled him? He could recall Ben hinting: *hadn't Regan's eyes turned silver on several occasions*? If only Ian had been in Camberlaune that night, that's what Ben had said to him. Repeatedly.

So, Ian had made Regan his scapegoat. But the last thing he could have handled at any point following the death of his sister, was admitting he'd been culpable. He wasn't proud of it, but there it was. His guilt had ruled him.

As he lay the entire situation out in his mind, one question arose. Why had he never doubted Ben's loyalty? Why had it never crossed his mind that Ben might be a traitor?

He had only to think back to the night of the massacre and he knew why. When Ben had found his brother's body, he'd gone wild with grief and had been completely inconsolable. And not just that night. Ben had been out of his mind for weeks.

Looking back, Ian knew Ben hadn't been putting on a show; his grief had been real. Ian could only suppose that whatever the nature of his plans, which had included the murder of his brother, the reality afterward had been something entirely different. Ben had experienced real pain for what he'd done and had been a wrecked man for months, eyes reddened day after day. Ben had lost weight and muscle, something warriors should never do. Killing his brother had hurt Ben

Because Ben had been grief-stricken, Ian had thought they'd suffered in the same way. Now Ian realized how wrong he'd been. Feeling bad after the fact was a far different cry from choosing *not* to commit a treasonous, murderous act in the first place. Ian's view of Ben had always been slanted by the depth of Ben's grief. He'd misinterpreted the signs completely and had placed his absolute faith in Ben. Now Ben had control of Regan.

Ian had little doubt as well that if he had continued to see Regan after the massacre, Ben would have found some other means of forging a divisive wall between them. Maybe he would have continued killing off more Camberlaune Realm-folk until Ian's guilt sent Regan away. Or maybe he would have simply had her killed.

And all this time, Regan had been guilty of only one thing: Loving him to the point of madness, just as she'd said.

Slowly, Ian rose from the deck. Something profound shifted within him in that moment. Maybe he'd run from Regan all those years ago because of his guilt about what had happened at Raven's Overlook, but he wouldn't anymore. He realized now that if he'd stuck with Regan, instead of shunning her as the problem, Ben's treachery would have long since risen to the surface.

He had no doubt Ben believed he'd won now that he had Regan in his clutches. But every bone in Ian's body knew differently. He was going after Ben and nothing would stop him.

The only question that remained was how to find Ben.

He began to pace again, yet this time he refused to allow guilt to swamp him. Instead, new ideas began to flow.

His thoughts turned toward Regan and how she'd doggedly worked to find the counter-spell by understanding Margetta's initial spell. She'd analyzed it and broken it down into several parts. She'd focused on only that, until she'd found the right formula.

He needed to do something similar. He turned his attention therefore to Ben. He was the key. Even if the Ancient Fae was involved, Ian only needed to analyze Ben in order to discover where he would have taken Regan.

And he knew exactly where to start.

Rising swiftly into the night air, he flew east in the direction of his Communication Center.

Chapter Ten

Regan had a battle going on within her mind as Ben drank from her wrist. She wanted and needed him because she was a blood rose, but her heart lived elsewhere and beat now with a fire she knew as Ian.

She loved Ian. She always had and this time with him, as transient as it had felt at the beginning, had only deepened her love.

She felt foolish in a way she couldn't explain, as though centuries of separation hadn't mattered one whit in how she really felt, would always feel.

But the blood rose in her was fixated on Ben, only on Ben, on resolving forever his chronic blood starvation, on making him stronger as a vampire and a warrior, on taking him into her body.

Desire for him flowed in tempting waves until she could hardly breathe. Thank the Goddess Margetta had left, but the Ancient Fae had said something about regrouping and had vanished. She hadn't levitated and left by the front door; she'd simply disappeared, as Davido and Vojalie could, another sign of the woman's power.

And again, Regan had the sense Margetta wasn't worried, as though she had plans in place that no one could defeat. The only thing she'd asked is that Ben get rid of Ian for good. Ben had made it clear he had no other intention.

But Regan had to do something or she knew how this time would end, especially since she could already feel Ben's mating vibration probing to gain entrance within her chest. Once he did, once his energy touched hers, she felt pretty certain she wouldn't be able to resist her overwhelming need to give herself to him completely.

As Ben groaned and suckled at her wrist, she dove deep, falling into the upper portion of her meditative state. She couldn't go completely because she needed to stay in tune with Ben's moment-to-moment intentions and to take action against him when necessary.

Goddess help her. She was in serious trouble.

And where was Ian? Could he ever find her?

~ ~ ~

A few minutes after leaving the Dauphaire Mountains, Ian arrived at the Communication Center in Somerstrong. The city was one of the largest in Camberlaune, built along both banks of the Peralin River. Lights glimmered from dozens of restaurants and shops fronting the broad stretch of water.

He made his descent, landing by the front door. Once inside the center, the staff turned toward him with warm greetings. He put on his most casual face, not wanting to give anything away. He needed information and he was pretty sure a series of direct questions wouldn't yield the results he was hoping for. Ben had chosen the Communication Center workers personally and each man here was loyal to him. As much as he wanted to lay it all out and explain what Ben had been up to, it would take way too long.

He gave them some details about the battle at Margetta's fortress and the subsequent evacuation of most of her army before the combined forces could engage. He added that he and Stone had a plan to bring all the mastyrs together to develop a major offensive against the Ancient Fae.

The staff, made up of three fae and a garrulous troll named Scott, gave shouts with fists raised.

When they'd settled down, he began his real inquiry with a ruse. "I'm working on a celebration feast for some of my staff with Ben as the guest of honor. He's been an incredible asset to me over the years, as you all know, but I want to keep this on the down low. Can you promise to keep my visit here a secret as well as anything else we might discuss?"

An effusive rush of 'yes, mastyr' followed.

"Good." All three waited in anticipation. "I'm thinking an event at the Hungry Troll. How does that sound? And free beer."

Another shout, along with nods of agreement and a couple of 'hell, yeahs', followed.

For the next few minutes, he chatted about the arrangements. Seeing their eagerness and how relaxed each was, he added, "By the way. Any of you know where Ben is right now? He took off from the gorge saying he had business at one of his homes and I've been to each but can't find him. I don't suppose he's checked in?"

Each shook his head, except for Scott who had compressed his lips and looked ready to burst with information. Trolls excelled at gossip.

Ian didn't go to him first. Instead, he kept fishing. "I know he has a townhouse here, a small farm near Clarefield and a beach cottage to the south. Anywhere else I could look, maybe someplace few people know about?"

The three fae shrugged their shoulders.

Scott's face had turned bright red from withholding information. For trolls, the sharing of any kind of news or details was one of the great pleasures in life.

Ian didn't press him, not in front of the others. Instead, he headed to the door. "I'm not too concerned. When he shows up, tell him to give me a shout."

He moved into the hallway, but only a few feet, and pretended to be checking emails on his cell. He was pretty sure the troll wouldn't be far behind.

The door to the Communication Center creaked open and Ian lifted his gaze to Scott. The troll closed the door behind him, then tip-toed over to Ian. He cast furtive glances left and right, but the hall was deserted. Scott would have made a terrible spy.

Ian held his gaze. "I suspected you might have something to tell me."

The troll bounced from one foot to the next. "It's something I figured out a while back. A friend of mine does contract work around Mercata and got a call to work on a property just north of there in the mountains. At first he wouldn't tell me who his client was."

"And you learned it was Mastyr Ben?" Ian was pretty sure Ben would have wiped the workers' minds the last day of construction. Ian said as much to the troll.

Scott's head bobbed. "Here's the thing. My friend let Ben's name slip over a couple of pints just two days before Mastyr Ben took care of his memory. I've remained silent, because Ben ought to have his privacy." He then shifted his gaze away from Ian and chewed on his thick lower lip.

"There's more, isn't there? As in you might know how to get there?"

Scott nodded, but this time he looked guilty as hell.

Ian patted his shoulder. "I won't tell Ben how I found his home, I promise. But I really need to talk to him. It's about Margetta, something he should know."

With the mention of the Ancient Fae and a hint this might have something to do with the ongoing war, Scott's expression lightened. "I followed him home one night," he confessed. "I know it was wrong. But when he took his car instead of flying, I couldn't help myself." Very troll.

Ian addressed the only important issue. He knew where Mercata was, but he wanted confirmation. "So, we're talking the Venaset Range?"

"Yes. Not far from the hamlet of Warrejet." He then gave detailed directions that sent Ian's heartrate skyrocketing.

"Don't worry about Ben. I won't reveal my source. Okay?"

When Scott returned to the center, Ian levitated along the hall then shoved the front door wide. He hit the skies once more.

He couldn't remember the last time he'd told so many lies. Not that he cared. Right now, he needed to get to Regan before Ben bonded with her. Nothing else mattered.

He flew as fast as he could to the east, to Mercata. But what would he find once he arrived?

~ ~ ~

Sitting on the side of Ben's bed, Regan worked hard to hold her meditative state. She found that as long as she stayed there, she was impervious to the bond Ben was attempting to forge.

The problem was he'd taken to hurting her in an attempt to bring her back.

He slapped her again, hard across the face. She fell to her side, then righted herself, yet somehow her meditation held. Ben's mating vibration once more flowed through her body, hunting for hers. But the meditation allowed her to keep it hidden.

For the moment, she was safe but it was only a reprieve. Each strike of his hand became more painful, more jarring. She knew it wouldn't be long before he discovered that with enough force he could disrupt her concentration completely.

At the same time, she had to battle her own powerful desire to rise like a geyser and embrace Ben with both arms. The urge, because she was a blood rose, was nearly overwhelming. She'd felt the same way with Stone when he'd arrived unexpectedly at Ian's gorge house.

Ben's voice rolled through the room. "Come back to me, Regan. I don't want to hurt you, but I need you."

The core of her being shuddered with a compulsion to do what he asked of her. Regardless, she remained very still, keeping her mind quiet, and sublimating her blood rose drive.

The next blow was so hard, however, she fell off the side of the bed and landed face down on the floor. He straddled her next then pulled on her hair, forcing her head up and back.

The combination of factors, of having been struck to the floor and the agony of her hair being pulled had its effect. Her meditative state vanished. She was fully present in the bedroom now and his mating vibration hummed deep inside her chest.

When her own mating frequency responded, she cried out telepathically. *Ian, help me! I can't hold out any longer.*

Because she'd used telepathy, Margetta's spell struck as though an axe severed her skull. She screamed in pain.

~ ~ ~

Ian heard Regan's telepathic cry for help at the same moment he arrived at the Venaset Mountains. He doubled his speed, whipping through the troll's directions. He found Ben's driveway set back from the main road, just as Scott had described it.

When he levitated about fifteen feet up the drive, however, he felt a powerful compulsion to turn and leave the property. A spell prevented any Realm-person from simply walking up to the house. He couldn't see much of anything, either, except a lot of forest. He felt confused as well, more indications a spell was at work.

Ian again remembered Regan's method of deep focus. He closed his eyes, and forced himself to continue up the hill. He brought his battle energy forward and faced his palms toward what felt like a tangled net of a spell. He thought it surprising he could discern the nature of the formula, almost thorny and angry, but with numerous holes. He'd learned a lot from Regan.

He had the impression that whoever had concocted this spell had been pissed off and in a hurry. He realized then just how much he'd shared with Regan when she'd broken down Margetta's spell.

As he centered his thoughts on the spell, he discovered its weakness and he brought his battle energy flowing into his right palm.

Opening his eyes, his mind once more felt confused as though he didn't know what he was looking at. But that was a result of being in the middle of the spelled territory. He opened his hand and fired a quick array toward the thorny spell.

He watched as his blue battle energy popped and sparked in several places, sending smoke into the air.

When the rest of Ben's driveway came into view, Ian knew he'd broken the spell.

He flew swiftly up to the house.

Before he even opened the front door, he heard Regan's screams. His fangs emerged as he followed the sound of her pain to what was a back room, probably a bedroom.

He shoved the door wide.

When he saw Ben sitting astride Regan, pulling on her hair, a red hue of rage covered Ian's eyes. Ben looked euphoric as well, a strong clue that he was a split-second away from forging the blood rose bond with Regan. He could sense both their mating bonds swirling and tightening.

He levitated then flipped to a horizontal position. He flew above Ben, caught his shoulders, pulled him off Regan and slammed him into the wood bedframe. Ben slumped sideways, though lifting his head and shaking it.

Ian returned to Regan, intending to pick her up and get her out of there. But the next moment, Ben was on him and had Ian in a choke hold.

Ian thought he'd be able to break free easily since he had more essential muscle mass than Ben. But he caught the scent of Regan's blood and knew that it now flowed through Ben. He was powered as never before.

Ian grabbed Ben's arm, but he couldn't break the hold on his neck.

The next thing he knew, Regan was in front of him, her hands settled on his forearms. Power surged through him. A moment later, she quickly backed away, tucking herself next to the bedside table.

Ian stepped forward with his right foot and at the same time, twisted slightly. Using his left elbow, he smashed into Ben's ribs.

Ben loosened his grip, grunting in response.

Ian grabbed Ben's left arm, and using his fangs, ripped into his muscle and tore out a chunk of his forearm.

Ben shouted in pain, then levitated backward several feet almost to the wall by the bathroom. He held his arm with his other hand, clearly healing the wound. He was doing it fast, too, another powerful side effect of Regan's blood.

After a moment, Ben lowered his shoulders and knees, getting into a combat position once more.

Ian spoke to Regan. "Get yourself someplace safe. I'll finish this."

Regan moved swiftly to stand near the door by the dresser, but she didn't leave. "I'm not going anywhere. We'll see this through together."

He could tell she meant it, but what she thought she could do, he couldn't imagine.

"Need a woman's help?" Ben sneered.

For a moment, Ian got lost in the thousands of memories of the man in front of him. He didn't recognize this version of Ben, the dark look in his eye, the way his nostrils flared, the cruel line of his mouth. "Were you pretending all those years? By all the elf lords, I never knew you."

"No, you didn't. You ruled Camberlaune. You never thought about me or what my life was like constantly in your shadow. Women flocked to you and gave me a cursory glance because I didn't have your weight, your power."

"You've done all this because of jealousy? How many have you had murdered, Ben, solidifying your position?"

A diabolical expression descended on his features, his eyes red-rimmed and bright. "Over a thousand, counting all the realms. And one more tonight."

Ben launched, a blur of motion Ian barely saw coming. Because of the strange movement, Ian knew some other force was at work.

Another spell.

Ben slammed into his chest this time, forcing Ian hard against the bedside table. Ben lifted Ian up with a hand beneath his arm, then punched him in the face repeatedly with his right fist.

Ian's head jerked back with each blow. He couldn't breathe and his brain was a mess because of the spell. But he'd been a warrior a long time and swept his leg behind Ben, knocking him off balance. As a result, Ben let go of him and fell to the floor.

The room was small for two big bodies. Ian moved toward the foot of the bed as Ben lifted up off the floor, levitating. Ian saw a flash of something, but he didn't know what it was. Shit, did he have dagger on him?

Once more, Ian's head grew clouded because of the added spell and he didn't see Ben coming until Ian felt a cut across his abdomen.

He looked down. Ben had sliced him, yet didn't penetrate the muscle, though he could have.

"I'm taking you down, Ian, one cut at a time. And I'll enjoy every second of it."

Ian stumbled as he saw the blur once more. He felt a burn over his right shoulder, then his left. But his mind wasn't working at all.

The next cut was low at his waist. He didn't even see movement of any kind this time. He dropped to his knees. "Regan … run."

~ ~ ~

Regan had been right not to leave. Ben had activated a latent spell, something with Margetta's signature all over it.

She'd dropped into her meditation with the first cut of Ben's dagger. She'd had no doubt what would happen next since the spell was messing with Ian's mind and making it impossible for him to function.

She could feel the formula, its intricacies and again its beauty. But she didn't have time to construct a counter-spell. Ian would be long dead before she could lift the veil of the spell so that Ian could battle Ben on an equal footing. With so much blood already pouring out of him, he'd be too weak to fight.

Ian had dropped to his knees holding his stomach as Ben moved in behind him. He slid a hand beneath Ian's chin, exposing his throat. He brought the blade up to his neck, smiling. She barely recognized the monster ready to kill a man he'd known for centuries and fought beside almost as long.

She couldn't let Ian die, but what could she do? She remembered what it had been like to share the blood tattoos with him. Each time he'd battled, she'd been with him and had felt how he did what he did. On instinct, she warmed up her battle frequency.

She centered herself on his warrior-ness and without giving it too much thought levitated, then rolled in the air in order to come up behind Ben. At the same time, she brought her battle energy into her palm. The moment she made contact with Ben's skull, she let her power flow.

He hadn't expected the blow. He turned toward her, a surprised look in his eye, then crumpled unconscious to the floor, his knife still gripped in his hand.

Regan dropped down beside Ian who sat on his knees and leaned against the bed. His complexion was pale and his eyes were closed. Blood poured from his cuts. She checked his throat first, but she'd been in time; there was only a small wound.

He would live.

For now, she focused on bringing forward her healing energy and letting it flow. But just as his wounds were almost sealed up, a golden light suddenly filled the bedroom and it wasn't good.

"What the hell is this?" Margetta shouted. "Ben just pathed me saying he'd taken Ian out."

Regan shrugged. "Guess he didn't count on me."

Margetta narrowed her eyes, her lips curling in disgust. "The only thing I hate more than an imbecile is a smart ass."

The Ancient Fae lifted a white hot palm to Regan. "Now let's find out which hurts more, the spell in your head or my battle power."

~ ~ ~

Ian came to full consciousness abruptly because Regan was screaming. She was in pain. He opened his eyes a little, but didn't move. He needed to know what kind of attack was in progress before taking action. Was Ben hurting her?

But the golden light he could see told him it was worse than that. Margetta was here.

And he couldn't path Regan because of the spell still shielding her telepathic abilities.

He forced himself to ignore the level of pain Regan was in and once more modeled her meditative process in order to quickly analyze the situation. More importantly, he only had a few seconds to figure out what to do.

His own pain, since he was still healing, he ignored.

That's when he felt something touching his chest, a vibration so at odds with the external battle, he wasn't sure he understood what it was.

Then he knew: Regan was sharing her mating vibration, touching his chest, asking for entrance. And she had a very specific plan in place.

Brilliant!

His corresponding frequency rose almost without having to form the thought. He also knew what this meant: he'd be forging a bond with her, the blood rose bond. With it, they'd each gain a tremendous boost in power.

For a couple of seconds, he hesitated. He wanted to ask her if she was sure. But he knew Regan. She wouldn't have come to him like this without having already made up her mind.

And more than anything else in the world, he wanted to bond with her.

He opened himself wide. The moment his vibration touched hers, he let his love for her flow, all that he'd held back for such a long time. Despite her physical agony, her mating vibration hummed against his, getting stronger and stronger.

He could feel the bond begin to form, a tightening of his energy with hers. His mind filled with an extraordinary light until at last the frequencies joined and the bond solidified. The same light exploded within his mind, power flowing through him in massive bursts.

He heard a shrieking sound and recalled that while Margetta was the Ancient Fae, she was also part wraith and had assumed that form now.

He opened his eyes and rose up. Margetta hung in the air, a wild, euphoric expression on her face. She was in her wraith form, wearing the traditional gown of red gauze. Gold streams of her battle power flowed over Regan, causing her enormous pain.

Regan's body was lit with a red aura, a sign she was battling Margetta in her own way, but with limited success. Margetta could have killed her outright that much Ian could see. Instead, she was taking pleasure torturing the Ruby Fae.

He let his battle energy ride across his shoulders then flow down both arms. He knew in that moment, because of his bond with Regan, he could kill the Ancient Fae.

Margetta shifted suddenly to stare at him, her eyes wide with shock.

He aimed his blue battle power at her, opening his palms wide. But the moment he fired, the golden light vanished. Margetta had disappeared. Which meant the energy he'd just released exploded the wall opposite him as well as the bathroom beyond.

He quickly covered Regan with his body, protecting her as debris landed all around them.

~ ~ ~

Regan couldn't believe what it was like to have Ian's frequency connected to hers. Power flowed, for one thing, so that she felt lit on fire. And the pain Margetta had been causing disappeared completely.

As the dust settled and Ian rose up, she followed, turning to stare at him. His dark gray eyes also seemed as fiery as she felt. She gripped his forearms and felt his power pulsing as though they still shared the blood tattoos.

"Ian, is this what you wanted? The bond, I mean?"

He drew her into his arms. "Being connected to you like this is exactly what I want. I love you. I always have."

She slid her arms around his neck and held him close.

After a moment, her gaze drifted to the floor. Ben was on his stomach, half buried in debris.

"Oh, sweet Goddess, is he dead?"

Ian released her and went to Ben. She watched him push some of the drywall and tile away from his body, then lean down to check for a pulse. "He's gone."

"Ian, I didn't mean to kill him. I saw where the battle was headed and because I'd fed him, I knew he had too much power. I swear I didn't mean to hurt him that bad. Just to incapacitate him."

Ian returned to her, pulling her close once more. "I'm sorry, Regan. I know this isn't what you wanted."

She drew in a ragged breath. "It's horrible. All of it. And he was so close to forging the bond with me."

A shudder passed through Ian. "Let's get you out of here. I'll contact Stone and let him take care of this. I know he won't mind taking charge."

She wanted to respond, but couldn't. Tears had started to flow and wouldn't stop.

~ ~ ~

Ian led Regan slowly through the house, an arm around her waist, her head pressed to his shoulder and chest. He knew she was weeping and he let her be.

When he tapped Stone's telepathy, the brother responded, *Tell me you got him.*

We did.

And Regan?

She's fine. Ian then related all that had happened, including the newly formed bond between himself and Regan.

When he told Stone he needed him to take care of Ben's body, Stone responded, *Give me the location and I'll be there as fast as I can. I'm in the air already, heading east with five of my best Guardsmen.*

As Ian shared the same directions Scott had given him, he walked Regan out onto the front walkway. He didn't stop there but kept her moving in the direction of the street away from the house. Though she trembled and his tank grew damp with her tears, all he felt was tremendous relief. He had her with him and she was safe from a man he now considered a sociopath and a monster.

He waited at the bottom of the long drive for Stone. The brother arrived a minute later with five powerful Guardsmen in tow.

Stone clapped him on the shoulder. "We've got this, Ian. Go. Take care of your woman."

Ian nodded. He felt blasted up one side and down the other from the events of the past few minutes.

As Stone and his men headed up the drive toward the house, Ian settled Regan on his boot, slid his arm tight around her waist, and once more headed into the night sky.

At first he wasn't sure where to go, except that he needed to be alone with her. In the end, he decided to take her back to his cabin near Juniango.

On the way, he pathed his caretaker and was told provisions had already been taken to the cabin. The man's wife had made an excellent leek and potato soup and a loaf of savory rosemary bread.

A few minutes later, when he landed on the front porch, Regan finally lifted her head. "I'm glad you brought me here."

"You've been through hell, so tell me what you need and I'll do it. Anything."

~ ~ ~

What Regan wanted most was a hot bath and some time alone to heal. Ian led her to his master bedroom, giving her the space she needed. Though she told him she was fine, a worried frown never left his brow.

A few minutes later, as she sank into the warm water, she let out a painful sigh. Part of her was euphoric from the unexpected bond. But another part was hurt in ways hard to quantify, as though the act of releasing her battle energy straight into Ben's head, had stripped something from her soul.

She'd never killed a fellow Realm-person before and she hoped more than anything else in life she never had to again.

But in that moment, when she saw how simple it would be to take Ben unawares and save Ian's life, she'd moved in and released her power. But the level of it had been greater than she'd realized. She'd thought she was streaming only enough to knock him out. Instead, it had been a killing blow.

She drew her knees up to her chest and wept anew, uncertain how long it would be until she felt like herself again.

Later, when a knock sounded on the door, she called out for Ian to come in. He didn't, however. Instead, he asked if she was all right. When she said she was, he offered her soup and a lot of wine.

She smiled. "Both sound great."

Her wounds had healed and she knew in time she'd come to forgive herself for the accidental death. She wasn't sorry Ben was gone, only that she wished he'd lived to be put on trial and his acts exposed for the treasonous murders they were.

~ ~ ~

Sitting on the deck, Ian held his third bottle of beer in his hands. He clinked his thumb ring against the glass, the sound oddly soothing. He'd wanted to shut off his vampire hearing because he'd heard Regan weeping. But he'd forced himself to listen and to acknowledge her suffering. In that way, he could honor the sacrifices she'd made tonight.

She appeared in the doorway, then moved toward him. "Hey, I can feel you thinking all the way in the bedroom." Her light brown hair was damp and hanging down her back. She wore a soft-looking blue sweater, blue jeans and no shoes.

Love for her rushed through his body, which caused a vibration to pass through their joined mating frequencies.

She put a hand to her chest. "That feels so strange. Wonderful, but strange."

He rose to his feet swiftly, then set the bottle on the table by his chair. "How you doin'?"

"Better. I think I'm in shock." Tears touched her eyes again.

He forced himself to take a deep breath. He ached inside his chest as though hands had grabbed his heart and squeezed. Hard. "Regan, I'm so sorry. Words … hell, I don't know what to say. I misjudged everything."

"I didn't see it, either," she said, her eyes now swimming with tears. "I would never have believed anything so bad of one of your Guardsmen and especially not Ben. I mean, I've never been completely easy around him and at times could feel something was off with him, but never this."

He took a step toward her. "I was so wrong." He put a hand to his chest, his own eyes burning. "Sweet Goddess, he was my best friend."

"Oh, Ian." Tears flowed down her cheeks as she moved quickly toward him.

He opened his arms and she fell against him, sobbing once more. *I can't stop crying. I think this is going to hurt for a very long time.*

I think you're right.

She slid her arms around his waist, holding him tight. "All those people. Your sister, too. It was the worst night of my life at Raven's Overlook."

"Mine, too. I lost so much. I lost you, my nieces, my sister and her good, decent husband, even Ben's older brother, and all because …" He couldn't say it. The reality was too raw, too painful.

She squeezed him tight. "Don't think about it right now."

"Hard to think about anything else." He rubbed her back, loving the feel of her against him, remembering what it had been like after the massacre to sleep in an empty bed. He'd felt hollowed out for years afterward. Now here she was, in his arms.

And they'd bonded.

"Regan." He had to ask. "I know the battle forced the bond between us and now I don't know what to say. I know how I feel about it, but—"

She drew back and caught his face with both hands. "How *do* you feel, Ian? I need to know."

His chest shuddered. "Regan, I love you. I've always loved you. Every woman I ever met had to live up to you and they couldn't. It's always been you."

She searched his eyes. "You're afraid, though. I can feel it. But of what?"

"That you won't be able to forgive me, even though we now share the blood rose bond. I treated you badly. I thought the worst things about you and let you know it. I don't deserve to be this close to you, ever."

For reasons he didn't understand, she smiled and more tears brimmed in her eyes. "Ian, all is forgiven. You have to believe me. Since we've been together these last couple of nights, and maybe even before when I helped Zane and Olivia defeat Margetta in Swanicott, I've gotten a better glimpse at what the ruling mastyrs have had to endure. That's one reason I can let it all go now. You gave me up to save Camberlaune and I know what it cost you. I also know that if you hadn't built a wall of blame between us, we would have come back together one day and Ben wouldn't have hesitated to act against us."

Ian nodded slowly. "You're right. He couldn't allow someone so powerful into Camberlaune. And eventually, given your fae insight, you would have seen him for what he was."

She drew a deep breath. "But I have to know, are you regretting the blood rose bond?"

"No. Sweet Goddess, no! Don't think it for a second. It's everything I've wanted but felt I could never have."

"Really?"

"Yes, but what about you? Do you feel you've made a mistake? Do you wish the bond undone?"

~ ~ ~

Regan wanted to tease him, wanted to tell him, 'too late now'. But she knew he needed reassurance. Guilt had dogged him on every front and she didn't want it to have an effect on them as they moved forward together. "I refuse to think of anything that's happened as a series of mistakes, including the bond. For me, this is my destiny, one I've craved since we were together so long ago. I don't in any way feel cheated because we chose to engage the bond in the heat of battle. Instead, I feel incredibly fulfilled. I mean, look what we were able to do? We ended Ben's secretive hold on Camberlaune and removed a powerful ally from Margetta's army. These are no small things.

"And to be honest, even if I didn't love you as I do, saving Camberlaune alone would have been worth it."

"You mean everything you just said, don't you?"

She arched a brow. "When have I ever lied to you?"

At that, a smile disrupted his somber, dark look. "Never. You've always told it to me straight and kept pushing back, even when I blamed you."

She hugged him, then pathed, *I love you so much and I love that we're bonded.*

When she drew back, his eyes were full of affection as he settled his lips on hers. The kiss warmed her heart, her mind and her soul. She became acutely aware of the way their mating vibrations now moved as one, sending pulses of love through her body.

After a moment, Ian drew back, but still held her tight. "There is something I want to be clear about. Saying good-bye to you back then hurt for years afterward. You were everything to me. It's my deepest regret, pushing you away."

"Ian, throughout all these centuries, you've had one of the toughest jobs around, all the ruling mastyrs have. I didn't like what happened after the massacre. But I came to understand that Raven's Overlook destroyed a part of you that my love could never have rebuilt. Even if we'd stayed together, you would have felt guilty the whole time."

He stared at her for a long moment, then said quietly, "I think you're right."

"So we're good?" she asked. She needed a lot of reassurance herself.

He nodded. "The bond feels so right to me and I love you more than words can ever express."

With her fears allayed and after one long, beautiful kiss, he offered her a meal. She took him up on it and savored the rosemary bread, flavorful potato soup, and glass of sweet German wine.

Later, with the dishes cleaned up, she took him out onto the deck. She had an idea about what she wanted to do next, but she wasn't sure he'd go for it.

She leaned into him, caressing his face and rubbing a thumb over his lips. "We have some lost time to make up for, don't we?"

"Yes we do. A mountain of it."

"I know this may sound irreverent, Ian, but I'd love to go to your cave right now. I know you've had women there, probably lots of them. But this has been a rough night and what I want needs to continue in that theme, though in a good way.

He rocked his hips into hers. "Rough like this?"

Her eyes fluttered. "Exactly like this. The only question remains, how fast can you get me there?"

His eyelids fell to half-mast. "As I recall, I could always get you there *fast.*"

She gasped, remembering. "You're a wicked man. But the way you could use your vibrations ... "

"Several places at once as I recall. So, how about we see if we can do it again?"

~ ~ ~

Ian took her into the air and focused on the small lake in the south of his realm, set in the middle of a series of low, green hills. He'd discovered and purchased the cave a couple centuries back, which meant Regan had never seen it before. He'd bought the surrounding land at the same time.

He also knew all sorts of rumors abounded concerning his activities in the cave, most of which weren't true. But he didn't waste his time trying to correct them. He was pretty sure he'd only add fuel to the fire if he made the attempt.

When the hills appeared on the horizon, he dipped and dropped down through the external opening that angled off the side of the westernmost hill. He descended slowly, turning Regan so she could see the sight below.

"It's an underground lake." She sounded surprised. "With a beach. How on earth did that happen?"

"I confess I had the sand shipped in."

"Smart thinking and the water is so clear. Can we swim?"

"Of course. Anything you want."

He flew her down to the edge of the water, descending to the sand. She stepped off his foot and got rid of her boots. He couldn't recall the last time he'd seen her move so fast as she stripped out of her clothes.

She ran into the water and once she was knee deep, she dove. The last thing he saw were the two mounds of her bottom as she disappeared beneath the water. A moment later, she resurfaced thirty feet farther in.

"I was right to have you bring me here," she called back to him. "There is something so cleansing about water."

He took off his boots, leathers and tank then followed her lead, wading in and diving. Once in the water, he swam to her before he surfaced. Reaching her, he caught her in his arms, but didn't stop there. Instead, he added levitation and carried her fifteen feet into the air.

"What are you doing?" But she was laughing.

He then turned her to face the water. "Plant your feet on my thighs then dive."

"Yes!"

He bent his knees and arched his hips so she could catch her balance. He stayed steady in the air, holding her at the top of her shins. When she was well-balanced, and probably using her own levitation as well, she hunched down, then launched. He added a bit of his own thigh-power to the dive, which sent her arcing into the air in a perfect swan-dive.

She surfaced, smiling and afterward levitated straight out of the water. She flew over to him and into his arms. His mating frequency vibrated heavily in his body, surrounding hers, a seduction all its own.

"Make love to me, Ian. That's what I want more than anything right now."

He looked into her face and saw her love for him, a connection he never believed would belong to him in this life. He kissed her, letting his love for her flow so that his entire body hummed with the promised vibrations.

She'd wanted to be in the cave and in the air. So, instead of taking her to the beach, he sustained them with his levitation and slowly leaned her backward. They were at least twenty feet above the water and another two dozen yards below the cave ceiling.

Once aroused and with the practice of centuries, he entered her body while in midair and began to move inside her. He realized she was levitating as well, her hips rocking into his in an erotic push back.

She surrounded him with her arms and kissed his throat. "I love you, Ian. So much." Her kiss turned into a nip. "But I want you to bite me while we do this."

He groaned as he drove into her. He paused just long enough to strike the vein at her throat. She cried out, her voice echoing in the domed chamber.

Her jasmine-lime flavor as well as her latent power flowed down his throat. The moment her life-force hit his stomach, his entire being lit up. Vibrations flowed everywhere, through their joined mating vibrations, along his arms and over his groin.

He'd never experienced anything so perfect in his long life. *How is this for you?*

~ ~ ~

Regan was ready to pass out from pleasure, certain she was about to die an extraordinary death. "Incredible," she whispered. Wherever he touched her his vibrations flowed into her, including his cock. And his lips on her throat as he drank from her kept her sex alive with desire.

She matched the thrusts of his hips, pushing back which gave him a solid place from which to drive into her again. Pleasure began to rise and sharpen. "Ian, come with me. I want you to come with me."

He left her vein, sealing the punctures with swipes of his tongue, then looking down at her. He held her loosely around her shoulders and moved his hips faster, his earthy forest scent adding another layer to all the sensations.

Ecstasy arrived on a tremendous wave. When he began to roar, she reached the pinnacle, her cries mingling with his. She savored the sound of Ian's release as it echoed around the cavern over and over. She felt as though she was listening to the birth of the universe, a great cataclysm of sound and power.

When the last of her pleasure drifted away and he'd released fully, he eased down, slowly levitating them both into the water. She caressed his face, loving the look in his eye of both wonder and adoration.

She felt the same way, caught up in the beauty of all that had happened between them. He floated her in the water for a few minutes, just holding her and whispering his love. Everything was changed and made new.

After a few minutes, she was ready to leave the cave. She turned into him and slid her arm around his neck, kissing him once on the lips. "All I want now is to return to your cabin and share your bed. How does that sound?"

"Like heaven."

~ ~ ~

Later, Ian led Regan back onto his deck to enjoy the last of the night. Because they were both naked, he'd wrapped them up in a comforter. The bond helped him to feel how content she was, and her contentment filled him with nothing short of joy.

When he'd brought her back to the cabin, he'd taken her to his bedroom and made love to her again. But it wasn't the quick, fiery lovemaking like at the cave. This time, he took it slow and with every touch, every kiss, every caress let Regan know how much she meant to him.

Now as he held her close, he couldn't believe so much love and meaning, so much power and yes, forgiveness, had come to him. He felt like a new man, someone who could move into the future with more to give his woman and his realm.

The woods were alive with night birds and the river rolled on and on. Stone had said they were meant to accomplish something together, but he'd never imagined it would be to uncover the treachery in his own realm. But in doing so, he'd also removed a formidable ally from Margetta's forces.

The Nine Realms was facing a critical turning point with the Ancient Fae. But Ian had a profound sense that the final showdown with Margetta would belong to Stone. Come nightfall, he would contact his fellow mastyr and offer to serve him in whatever way was needed.

For now, he savored what had been given to him. He felt blessed far more than he deserved. But he had enough sense not to refuse the bounty.

"I love you." He embraced Regan more fully and took pleasure in the way her whole body responded to him, moving in a slow sensual glide.

Still facing away from him, she reached up with her hand and caressed his face. "The blood rose bond is heaven."

"It is."

He didn't know what this was like for other mastyrs and their bonded blood roses. But for him, he felt as though he'd finally come home after a long, difficult voyage.

Regan was his home. That's what he knew. And from this point forward, through however many years would be given to them, she always would be.

Thank you for reading EMBRACE THE HUNT! In our new digital age, authors rely on readers more than ever to share the word. Here are some things you can do to help!

Sign up for my newsletter! You'll always have the *latest releases, hottest pics,* and *coolest contests*! **http://www.carisroane. com/contact-2/**

Leave a review! You've probably heard this a lot lately and wondered what the fuss is about. But reviews help your favorite authors -- A LOT -- to become visible to the digital reader. So, anytime you feel moved by a story, leave a short review at your favorite online retailer. And you don't have to be a blogger to do this, just a reader who loves books!

Enter my latest contest! I run contests all the time so be sure to check out my contest page today! Enter Now! **http://www. carisroane.com/contests/**

Also, be sure to check out the Blood Rose Tales – TRAPPED, HUNGER, and SEDUCED -- shorter works set in the world of the Blood Rose, for a quick, satisfying read.

BLOOD ROSE TALES BOX SET

http://www.carisroane.com/blood-rose-tales-box-set

BLOOD ROSE TALES BOX SET: http://www.carisroane.com/ blood-rose-tales-box-set/

TO PURCHASE THE BLOOD ROSE TALES SEPARATELY:

TRAPPED: http://www.amazon.com/Trapped-Blood-Tales-Caris-Roane-ebook/dp/B00I3OEDS0

HUNGER: http://www.amazon.com/Hunger-Blood-Tales-Caris-Roane-ebook/dp/B00J08CUO8

SEDUCED: http://www.amazon.com/Seduced-Blood-Rose-Tales-Book-ebook/dp/B00N6HHU8O/

About the Author

Hi, Everyone! I'm a USA Today Bestselling Author and I write super-sexy paranormal romance fiction designed to be as much an adventure as a soul-satisfying experience. With every book, I try to give a taste of real life, despite the fact that I'm writing about hunky vampire warriors. You'll come away engrossed in the lives of my vampires as they wage war, as they make love, and as they answer the tough questions of life in terms of purpose, eternity, and how to raise a family! I began my career with Kensington Publishing writing Regency Romance as Valerie King. In 2005, Romantic Times Magazine honored me with a career achievement award in Regency Romance. I've published twenty-nine paranormal stories to-date, some self-published and some for St. Martin's Press. To find out more about me, please visit my website!

www.carisroane.com

Author of

Guardians of Ascension Series – Warriors of the Blood crave the breh-hedden

Dawn of Ascension Series – Militia Warriors battle to save Second Earth

Blood Rose Series – Only a blood rose can fulfill a mastyr vampire's deepest needs

Blood Rose Tales – Short tales of mastyr vampires who hunger to be satisfied

Men in Chains Series – Vampires struggling to get free of their chains and save the world

Other Titles:

RAPTURE'S EDGE 1 AWAKENING
BLOOD ROSE SERIES BOX SET, featuring Book #1 EMBRACE
THE DARK and Book #2 EMBRACE THE MAGIC
EMBRACE THE DARK #1
EMBRACE THE MAGIC #2
EMBRACE THE MYSTERY #3
EMBRACE THE PASSION #4
EMBRACE THE NIGHT #5
EMBRACE THE WILD #6
EMBRACE THE WIND #7

BLOOD ROSE TALES BOX SET
TO PURCHASE THE BLOOD ROSE TALES SEPARATELY:
TRAPPED
HUNGER
SEDUCED

THE DARKENING
THE AWAKENING
VEILED
VAMPIRE COLLECTION (Includes BRINK OF ETERNITY)
WICKED NIGHT/DARK NIGHT (Boxed Set)

CPSIA information can be obtained
at www.ICGtesting.com
Printed in the USA
FSOW02n1102090217
30618FS